The Most Wanted

The Most Wanted

THE BANK ROBBERS BOOK 4

ANNIKA MARTIN

Reading order

The Hostage Bargain

The Wrong Idea

The Deeper Game

The Most Wanted

The Hard Way

The Best Trick

Chapter One

I was power lounging behind the front desk of our new private investigation office wearing a fabulous red Coco Chanel skirt suit.

Was I was overdressed? Maybe, but it was the first day we were open, and I wanted to set a professional tone. And hey, being able to wear nice clothes was one of the perks of being the significant other of three very successful bank robbers.

The suite of offices we'd chosen for our new P.I. firm was on the second floor of an awesome vintage building just off of one of the main drags in downtown L.A.

I loved it for the film noir appeal, what with its wooden floors and high ceilings.

My three clever and kinky lotharios loved it for the fire escape, the sight lines, and the easy roof access.

Because sure, this was a semi-legit business, but we were still wanted bank robbers who had to stay nimble and safe.

And of course some jerk of a police sketch artist had made the most dramatically unflattering police sketches of us possible.

But you can't exactly write a letter of complaint to the LAPD asking that they redo your sketch to have your eyes not so close together. At least, that's what Zeus was always telling me.

The larger threat and the real reason we needed quick escape routes was ZOX, the intelligence agency my guys used to work for. If ZOX showed up, there would be real trouble.

It was the one thing my hardened criminals were scared of. The only thing that kept them up at night. (Well, maybe not the only thing.)

As an added benefit, an office like this was nice for the thieves, gangbangers, hoodlums, hitters, and assorted fugitives of L.A. County. Most private investigation firms out there probably served coffee and bagels to their clients; we offered a convenient escape route, should they be tailed.

I will confess that I was surprised when Zeus first started talking about launching the P.I. firm—it's not like we needed the money.

He claimed he was bored, and that we needed something more beyond robbing banks. He got Thor and Odin excited about the challenge of using our skills to help criminals who didn't have access to effective investigative services. But was that really it?

I sensed there was more to it.

The door had one of those cloudy glass windows just like in old movies. There was some debate over what to paint on it. In the end, we left it blank, except for the office number. Again —discretion.

We were thinking about printing business cards, though we couldn't quite decide on a tagline for our agency. My suggestions included *Criminals need a detective agency, too!* and *To catch a criminal, you have to BE a criminal.* But Odin thought those ideas were a little too obvious. Thor wanted to just use our gang motto: *You WISH we were dead, motherfuckers.* But it didn't seem like the kind of thing you would want to put on a business card, considering their purpose was to attract clients, not frighten them.

Just in case you're wondering—no, Zeus, Thor, and Odin are

not their real names. My real name isn't Isis. The last time I used my real name was more than a year ago, back when I was their hostage during a robbery gone bad. Actually, the robbery went pretty well for me, though if I'd known how that day would end, I would've worn way better underwear.

And I would've hugged my sisters before I left the farm that morning for my bank job. I missed them so bitterly that sometimes I thought the feeling would consume me. I'd been dying of boredom in that old life, but I'd never imagined leaving forever, having to fake my own death to protect them.

I tried not to think about that.

So I waited there at my massive wooden desk, excited that our first client was arriving soon. I arranged the folders and made sure the word game and cartoon porn windows were closed on my laptop, just in case we had to research something in front of the client.

When I looked up next, there was Zeus, leaning in the door frame between our offices, arms crossed, which made his fine brown sport jacket pull tight over his massively muscular arms.

"I like that jacket," I said.

He didn't reply; he merely stood there, eyeing me like a dark predator.

My heart rate kicked up. The dark predator gaze...surely he wasn't thinking about sex at a time like this! All the same, I closed the laptop and slid it into a drawer. Because...experience.

In a movement more animal than human, he pushed off the door frame and moved toward me. He stopped in front of my desk, shrugged off the jacket, and set it beside the folders.

"I said I liked it. I didn't mean you had to give it to me."

"Goddess," he whispered hoarsely. He fingered the top button of his shirt, then flicked it open, revealing a triangle of man chest.

"Zeus. What are you doing?"

He held my gaze from across the desk as he opened another button.

I smiled. "Dude!"

He had that dark, wild look in his eyes that sometimes scared me but mostly turned me on. Something warmed in my belly as he undid button after button, until his shirt hung open, revealing the middle of his massive chest. He slid a hand over his washboard abs, making me imagine sliding my hand there, making me imagine the hard warmth of his washboard abs.

I looked at the small line of fur trailing down from his belly button, down, down…*Gah!!* I curled my fists, mentally beaming a message to my better self, my more responsible self. *Must not touch him. Client coming. Must…not…have…sex.*

Zeus pressed his hand between his legs.

My heart rate went double time, and my responsible self was getting so far away. "Our first client is coming at any minute." There was a Mr. Alexander Hamilton scheduled for nine o'clock.

"Do I look like I'm here to consult Google Calendar?" he asked.

My belly tightened as he toyed with the snap on his pants. I could see from the bulge that he was hard as steel, and I was suddenly wishing Mr. Alexander Hamilton had scheduled himself for ten instead of nine. Better yet, noon.

"Is this how a man consults Google Calendar?" Zeus asked again, voice roughened with lust.

"I don't know. In France, maybe?"

He moved his hand down, watching me steadily.

"He'll walk in at any minute," I said.

"Door's locked."

Somebody had to act professional here, and apparently that was me. "They'll see shapes moving around in here, and they'll hear. We should wait for after." I stacked my folders, heart pounding with excitement.

Zeus leaned over the desk. A sexy snarl played on his lush lips. With one massive tree trunk of an arm, he slid the folders onto the floor.

"Hey!" My skin tingled as I stared at the now-bare surface. "I was *doodling* on one of those."

"I need you, goddess," he grated.

I straightened the lapels of my suit, like my professional exterior would cancel out my wildly unprofessional desires. "*Clients*, Zeus. Haven't you ever heard 'you never get a second chance to make a first impression?' What kind of an impression does it make if a client walks in on us fucking?"

The door off to the side of the reception area opened, and Odin came in with a file cabinet. "What's going on?"

"A client's on the way," I began breathlessly, "and..."

"And the boss wants to fuck his secretary," Zeus said.

I bit back a smile. I wasn't really secretary—I was an equal partner in the gang and the firm now, too. But this was role-play secretary, one of our favorite games, and the fact that we were in an actual office was giving it an extra edge.

Odin set the cabinet down and came over to me, shaking his head sadly. "Ice."

"Our first client is coming any minute," I protested. *And my responsible self is moving out of communication range.*

Odin reached my side of the desk and stood over me, holding out his hand. "Goddess," he whispered. "If the boss wants you, the boss gets you."

My heart pounded. *Odin, too?*

And then a little voice added, *yay!*

Thor was gone today, working at the little clinic he ran over the border. Not that he'd put a stop to something like this.

Odin took my arm and hauled me up close so that I was nearly flush with his hard, warm body, making me tingle all over. In a harsh and utterly dominating whisper, he said, "The boss needs your panties. Now."

Part of me was thinking *yes*. But part of me was thinking about *Alexander Hamilton*...not that the founding fathers are the sexiest ever, but the musical was amazing and if you look at a ten-dollar bill, that Alexander Hamilton is also hot.

"What thoughts, goddess? Is something *distracting* you from your secretarial work?"

"Uh—"

"Now," Zeus commanded.

With trembling hands I reached under my skirt, pulled my panties down my legs, and stepped out of them, then snatched them up and dropped them in his outstretched palm. "Alexander Hamilton specifically asked for nine o'clock."

"That's the name our client gave?" Odin asked. "Alexander Hamilton? Yeah, that doesn't sound fake."

I shrugged. "It's not a bad name."

Odin put on a stern face now. "Boss needs you bent over the desk."

"There are people walking by, down the hall," I said, playing the part of the voice of reason, which always just made everything sexier. "They'll know, you know..."

"I don't care. I'm proud of our relationship," Zeus said, one lazy hand on his cock, hardening himself for me. "This is how we express our love for each other, and if anybody wants to act like it's wrong, I will fuck them up. I'll make them sorry."

He would, too. I couldn't help but remember a certain day spa that wouldn't give the four of us a couples massage. Zeus almost trashed the place.

"But there are seven other offices on this floor alone. What if our office neighbors hear?"

"I'll fuck them up, too," Zeus growled, being his typical unreasonable self, always looking to beat the crap out of anybody who criticized our foursome.

It turned me on a little.

Okay, a lot.

Zeus growled again, sensing the pleasure his words were giving me. He lowered his voice to a hoarse whisper. "I'll fuck them up."

My pulse raced. Yeah, it was probably wrong that it turned me on.

Let's just say that at this point, my responsible self was orbiting the moon. Possibly Uranus.

Odin pulled me close, flush with his body. The feel of his log of a cock against my belly sent a bolt of arousal through my core. He grazed my lips and cheeks with cinnamon-flavored kisses, just holding me there for a long time, forcing me to relax against him, to feel him.

Odin loved letting me feel his power and control. He was psychological ops back when the guys were badass covert agents. Back when they weren't being hunted by the agency they'd once worked for.

I was starting to forget about Hamilton.

Slowly, Odin slid his hands up the backs of my thighs. "We'll make it so good, baby." His hands continued up, rough and warm on my ass now. "Bend over the desk, face down. I suggest you perform your secretarial duties before the client arrives. You've earned five strikes for five objections. Are you going for a sixth?"

Strikes. A shiver sailed through me. "I didn't object five times."

"Now you get six," Odin said.

Odin pulled apart the lapels of my fire-engine-red jacket and located my nipples, rock-hard through my silk shirt. Lightly he began to twirl them.

I melted under his touch.

"Seven. Will you go for eight, goddess?" He rubbed bristly whiskers against my cheek as he rolled my nipple between his clever fingers. "Because I could really go for eight. I will make it *fucking-g* sing for you, baby."

Sensation spiked through my belly. I glanced at the clock. Maybe professionalism was overrated.

Odin smirked. "You like to be watched anyway. Maybe we'll make our new client watch."

"That would be a new twist on the concept of full service," I joked.

Zeus stroked his cock. "She only likes us to watch. She would never want a random stranger to watch."

"Never is a strong word," Odin said.

"But the right word," Zeus growled.

"Says who?" Odin asked.

"Me." Zeus said. "It's a no-go."

Odin frowned. He wasn't feeling Zeus's new no-go.

I was thinking about it. I definitely liked it when one of my guys watched the other two take me. A lot of times Thor was the watcher. Would it add to things to have a stranger watch? I imagined an edgy, unknown presence in the room, eyes invading me as Zeus and Odin ravished me. A dangerous stranger, silent in the corner, cold eyes on my vulnerable body as I got utterly dominated.

I was starting to like the idea.

I looked over to see Odin regarding me carefully. He smiled, like he was reading my mind.

Zeus came over to us, and I kissed him, but I couldn't get the stranger thing out of my mind—that was the evil of Odin and his psychological insight.

I wouldn't know what the stranger was thinking and that would give everything a sexy edge.

I'd like it best if the watching stranger was a stern, clean-cut, really authoritarian person.

And gravely disapproving. He would have to highly disapprove of us.

The stranger would need to be tied up, too—I wouldn't want the stranger to be able to jerk off, because that was too much like a new person having sex with us, and hey, I'm a three man gal!

The tied-up, stern, authoritarian stranger would be allowed to watch us fuck and *nothing more.*

Odin started back up with his mind-melting nipple twisting.

"You would like that, goddess, wouldn't you? Are you thinking about it?"

Zeus stopped kissing me. "She wouldn't like it."

Where did this tension between them come from? "A thing is only fun if we're all into it," I said.

"So you'd like it?" Zeus asked. "You were thinking about it, weren't you?"

"What are you, the thought police? I think a lot of things." I considered giving the Alexander-Hamilton-looking-sexy-on-the-ten-spot example, but I decided that would only hurt my case. "I was testing it in my mind, that's all."

Odin smiled. "And enjoying it."

Zeus frowned. "Isis, isn't what we have between us enough?"

"Of course it is!" I said.

Odin's gaze glittered. "But a watcher is different, isn't it, Ice? You'd like a stranger to watch. A menacing, silent stranger to add a little danger. You love danger, you love an edge."

Zeus frowned some more.

"It's not like that..."

Odin grabbed my hair and made me look into his amber eyes. "Do not lie."

My pulse skittered. I so wanted to fuck now.

"I'm not lying," I gasped. "I would never want to fuck anybody else except you guys—not ever!"

"But," he said.

I shrugged. "Watching is different."

Odin twisted my hair. His rough treatment of me made my sex feel electric. "How, goddess?"

My heart pounded. "Just never you mind."

"Stop stalling. How is it different? Describe it all." He twisted harder.

This mean-bosses game was starting to melt my mind—in a good way!

"Sort of...knowing somebody else's eyes are on us, like a stranger..." I trailed off.

"Ten spanks if you don't complete that sentence now," Odin said.

"I guess...it would increase the awesomeness of being with you guys. Just...*yum!*"

Zeus frowned. "There will be no watching."

Odin stiffened, and not in the sexy way. "That's not a rule you can make, Zeus."

"I'm making it now, Odin."

I looked back and forth between them. What was up with Zeus?

Odin was right. It wasn't the kind of rule Zeus could make. Zeus got to command things in any kind of military situation just because you needed a commander, but he didn't get to make everyday rules for the group. Thinking of new dirty things to do was one of our favorite activities.

Odin frowned and let go of my hair. "You can say you are making a rule, *Zeus*, but that doesn't mean—"

"Zeus isn't into it, so let's drop it," I said.

Odin turned to me. "But you would like our new client to watch."

"No!"

"Why not? Do you have to meet him first?" It was weird that Odin was ignoring Zeus's desires.

"I don't like this," Zeus said.

"I like it," Odin said. "You have a type for watching, Isis?"

"It's off the table," I said.

"What is your type for watching, goddess?"

I pushed him away. "This is ridic."

"A watcher is not happening." Zeus's tone was grave. Serious in a new way. This was big for him.

It was weird, because having a watcher was just a drop in our dirty activity bucket. Or more like, our dirty activity universe.

Was this the equivalent of a couple fighting about the cap getting left off the toothpaste because nobody wants to talk about the deeper issues?

"I know you have a type in mind," Odin said. "You are always very specific in your fantasies. You have an image—a full profile, perhaps. And I will get it from you." As government agents-turned-bank robbers, they got heavy into things like profiles.

I prayed Hamilton would hurry. "A kink is only fun if we're all into it."

"I want the profile."

Zeus said, "It doesn't matter because we're not doing it."

"And I don't know anyway," I lied.

Odin had my hair again. "Oh, goddess, you do know." He pulled me near, lips softly grazing the most sensitive spot on my neck. He snaked a hand around my belly and kissed my neck, and then he kissed my ear—an unfair place to kiss me, and he knew it. My knees began to shake, and still he kissed my ear, wet and warm, sending my responsible self clear into a different universe. Then, slowly, he pushed me down over the desk and held me there with my cheek squished against the smooth wood.

I heard Zeus stroll around to the other side of the desk. He came into view in front of me and started fingering the top button of his pants.

My senses began to tingle as Odin shoved up my skirt up roughly over my ass. "Help Zeus. Get his cock out."

Chapter Two

MY SEX HEATED WITH DELICIOUS WARMTH. ODIN WAS IN one of his directing moods.

I craned my neck to meet Zeus's stormy gaze, as best as I could from that position, then I pressed my small, pale hand over the massive bulge in his pants. Did he still want to fuck after that whole conflict?

"He still wants it," Mr. Omniscient said from behind me. "We will always want you. That is never in question."

I grabbed onto Zeus's steely bulge. He sucked in a breath.

"Scratch," Odin said. "Do it. He'll like that right now." I drew my fingernails over the placket of Zeus's pants. Out the corner of my eye I saw Zeus throw his head back. He groaned, reminding me of a large animal, helpless in the face of pleasure. I took that as a yes and began to undo his pants.

"Still, ten strikes for your lying, Isis. While you suck Zeus's cock."

"I wasn't lying," I squeaked. *More a fib?*

Odin leaned sideways on the desk next to me, still holding me down while I handled Zeus's cock. He watched me for a long time, reminding me of a snarling wolf, establishing domination. "You think I don't know when you're *fucking-g* lying?" He always pronounced his g's extra hard, part of his Moroccan accent, which always intensified when he was emotional. "I need to always know about you."

"You always need to know about everybody." I stroked Zeus's cock, feeling it swell in my grip.

Odin grinned his glittery grin.

"You know about the important things," I said.

"I need to know everything, and I'll decide what's important," Odin said.

"No watchers," Zeus growled from above us.

"But we can know about her tastes," Odin said. "All intelligence is worth having." I felt his warm, rough hand caressing my ass. He nudged me gently toward Zeus, and I went. "Slide up. Suck him, goddess."

The wooden desk was just wide enough that I could be bent over it with my ass hanging off one side and my head on the other, and it stood about cock height.

Which was a bit suspicious, come to think of it. I imagined the three of them at a furniture store trying to work out the logistics. Maybe a salesperson talking about the type of wood, while they were more about standing next to it, measuring the top with sex positions in mind.

"I need you to suck me, baby," Zeus whispered urgently. "I need you to just—just take me, baby."

I found it hot when one of my guys went all *I'll die if I can't have you right NOW goddess please please,* but the strangled tone of his voice and the way he moved his fingers on my hair...let's just say that Zeus was acting more like that than normal.

I grabbed him at the root. His cock was thick and mighty and sensitive, just like him, and I loved it like I loved him. I gave him a big lick, long and strong on the underside, really letting him feel it, and then I kissed the top to evilly tease him. He let out another strangled cry.

"He needs you, Ice," Odin said. "He needs you to take him in all the way."

"The client," I reminded them as I thumbed the glistening drop of precum off the tip of Zeus's cock. "Don't you want clients to take you seriously?" I made little circles over the head of his cock with my thumb, and Zeus groaned.

Okay, I wasn't exactly helping in the professionalism department. But hey, the guys were beyond being taken seriously in our community. They were the most dangerous motherfuckers around.

I squeezed him at the base.

"Fuck it," Zeus panted. "If they don't want to take us seriously, I'll pound their faces 'til they do."

"Wow, if this P.I. thing doesn't work out, you could just go ahead and give seminars on corporate image building."

Zeus stroked my hair, ignoring me. He really was kind of gone. "You are so beautiful, goddess. I want to do everything to you at once."

Odin slid off the desk and tucked my skirt up so that my ass was completely bare and exposed. He slid his warm, callused palm down one cheek and up another, all gentle and soft, but I knew all too well not to trust that.

I dragged my lips over the head of Zeus's cock, tensed for the moment when Odin would start hitting, but instead he kept up with the tender attentions. He dipped a finger between my legs, stroking through my folds.

I gasped, reeling at the intensity.

"You like that?" Odin asked.

"Yeah," I breathed.

"Louder."

"Yes," I squeaked. He dipped two fingers in, sliding and stroking between my legs.

Zeus disengaged himself from my busy little hand. He knelt down and kissed me, then he gazed into my eyes, stroking my cheekbone with the thick pad of his thumb. "You are aroused, goddess, but a little bit reluctant, aren't you?"

"Yes," I said, mind melting from Odin's increasingly creative and invasive fingers.

Zeus continued. "You know what that does to us? That fucking drives us wild. Odin is going to give you your punishment while you suck my cock. Be careful. No biting, understand?"

"It will just go badly for you if you bite," Odin said.

"When have I ever bitten?"

A flash of warning shone in Zeus's eyes.

Right then I felt Odin's hand come down on my ass, hard and merciless, leaving a stinging sensation vibrating through my entire pelvis. "Count."

"One," I gasped.

He hit again.

"Two," I said, stunned at how loud and hard the spanks were.

Zeus stroked my hair. "You know how important discipline is to us, baby," he said.

Whack.

"Three," I gasped.

Zeus was going on, stroking my hair, talking to me gently, doing the good cop/bad cop thing I sometimes got off on. "...perfect discipline...to our group."

"Yes," I breathed.

"You will continue to count as you suck Zeus's cock," Odin commanded.

"How?" I protested.

"You can do it, baby," Zeus growled, standing up, touching my hair. "I need your lips on me, goddess."

"You are so wet," Odin said, drawing his fingers in and out, sliding my juices all around. "So you have a type for watching?"

"Stop talking." Zeus fit my hand around the firm pole of his cock. He groaned as I closed my lips around the head. Odin slapped my ass again. The slap stung in the cool air, feeling hot and sharp.

I made a sound in my throat that was supposed to approximate four.

"Jesus!" Zeus tightened his fingers in my hair. "Oh, baby, that's good." Zeus pulled his cock out of my mouth and slowly pushed in again. I sucked and gripped hard. "Count more. More counting."

Odin hit again. I made another sound in my throat, a five, and I could feel Zeus's cock pulse with sensation. "Fuck," he said, thrusting.

Again and again Odin spanked me. I lost count, not that it mattered, because at this point I was just groaning every time he hit me and that seemed to suffice. I found my burly bandit most preferred a low, rumbly groan.

"*Uh-uh-uh,*" he said as he fucked my face. "I need you to take me all the way in, goddess." He pulled my hand from his cock and pushed deeper, slowly pushing into my throat. "Count like you were, baby. You have to keep counting."

I could feel the head of his cock pushing against the back of my throat.

Odin brought his wicked hand down on my ass once more. Again I groaned. Again Zeus groaned, grip tightening on my head.

I wished I could talk—Zeus was still being gentle, begging me to take him all, but I wanted to tell him to take *me* all, to use me. To have me. To consume me totally.

The spanking seemed to have stopped. Had it been eleven strikes already? I was so turned on I could barely think straight.

Odin pushed my thigh to the side, spreading me, and threw himself into stroking my pussy. "You are almost there, goddess," he grated.

Zeus was, too, now, all raw furious need, devouring me, fucking me. He seemed barely conscious of what he was doing, so gone with pure lust and need.

"*Uh-uh-uh,*" he said.

I felt the head of Odin's cock probing at my entrance. I found I desperately wanted him inside of me. He pushed in, just a tiny bit.

I made a strangled little sound, needing more.

"You must wait, goddess, while we take our pleasure." Odin grabbed hold of my thighs and spread me wide, spearing me slowly, filling me with every thick inch. I groaned again. He angled himself to hit my clit.

I whimpered—best I could, anyway, what with Zeus's cock filling my throat. It worked for Zeus, judging from the streak of profanity that tore from his mouth as he came. My eyes watered, tears tickling down my cheeks.

Odin caressed my back. "You could come right now, couldn't you, goddess?" He was fucking me relentlessly now. I whimpered again. Yes, I was going to come, there was no stopping it. Odin knew it. Odin always knew. "Take it, Isis," he growled. "Take it."

Zeus pulled out of me as Odin shoved in again, hitting me in that place that made the world explode behind my eyelids. I cried out.

"Yes," Odin whispered. "Come, goddess." I could feel him taking on the pistoning speed that told me he, too was coming. Zeus stroked my hair, kissing the back of my head. Odin came, then, loudly, clearly not caring if Alexander Hamilton was out there.

Eventually we all wound down.

Odin collapsed across my back, warming me. He slid his hands up my arms until he had my fingers knitted in his, closing my hands into fists inside his fists, and kissed the shell of my ear. "You know what you do to me?" he whispered, moving on me. "To us?"

I smiled to myself. I had a pretty good idea. I felt like the luck-iest woman in the world.

Footsteps. "Quick, get off her." It was Zeus. He pulled Odin off me. "Don't move, goddess."

I stayed there, cheek on the smooth wood of the desk. He was pulling my legs apart, so I assumed the *don't move* didn't apply to my legs, and I spread them obediently. I felt a warm washcloth being swiped between them, and then a soft towel, patting my pussy dry.

I smiled. I could do it myself, but it was nice to have all that crazy tenderness come out of a hard man like Zeus. And it was sometimes important for Zeus to do caring things, like it made him a little less psycho.

Three knocks on the door.

"Shit." I wriggled around, sitting up on the desk.

Hearing no answer, whoever was out there tried to turn the knob and open the door.

"Hold your fucking horses," Zeus growled.

"Shhh," I whispered, sliding off the edge. "Hold, please," I called, smoothing my skirt. *Hold, please?* Equally inane, considering they were at the door and not on the phone, but I'd just had that mind-splitting orgasm.

Zeus had the moist towelettes now. "I love you like this, goddess. Mascara dripping down your cheeks, lips coated with my cum, eyes glazed from coming. You are never more beautiful than when you're ravaged by our hard love."

"Thanks," I said. "Though I'm not sure if it's right for an everyday look."

He kept on, wiping my cheeks clumsily with the towelette.

"Gimme that." I swiped it from his hand and grabbed my compact mirror. Yeah, my cheeks were painted with sideways rivulets of mascara tear trails.

Zeus smoothed my bright blonde bangs to the side and finger-combed the front part while I fixed my face. "You are so beyond perfect, Isis."

"We need to improve our *fucking-g* customer service," Odin said, grabbing his own moist towelette.

"If they want fucking customer service, they can go to Starbucks," Zeus growled, cleaning up.

"Finally!" I whispered. "There's our tagline." I snapped my compact shut and lifted my hands, making an invisible space between them, like the words were written in the air for all to read. "Kinky Bank Robber Investigations. If you want fucking customer service, go to Starbucks."

I smoothed my hair and glanced at Odin.

"You look beautiful, goddess," he said, knowing my question before I'd asked it, as usual. He handed me my panties. I pulled them on.

When things seemed ready, I went over, unlocked the door, and opened it, stepping aside. I bit my lip as a way to hide my surprise when I saw who was there.

It was Herk Washington, one of the smartest, scariest badasses around, leader of a powerful up-and-coming gang—huge and highly organized.

"Welcome," I mumbled, extra glad that my face was now free of mascara and cum.

Chapter Three

Herk strolled in like he owned the place, all six and a half feet of him, shiny reddish- brown hair caught in a pony-tail. He wore a fine black suit jacket with a white shirt underneath, buttoned all the way up to his neck. He fixed his eyes on Zeus, pack leader to pack leader.

"Herk," Zeus said, holding out his hand.

Herk took it and grasped it.

I didn't really know Herk, but my guys liked and admired him. Even so, tension always went up in a place when Herk Washington entered. Half the drugs in Los Angeles ran through him and his people, and they were very, very capable people. Powerful people.

Rumor had it that Herk was running his sales organization with encrypted networks and managing it with Trello, creating enormous efficiencies. But all the apps in the world didn't keep a man from being lethal if you crossed him.

Or screwed up his case.

I knew we'd be dealing with dangerous people, doing investigations for the criminal underworld. But I never thought it would be somebody like Herk. It seemed to me that Herk could go around questioning people, and they'd just give up the answers purely out of fear. The man was reportedly as sensitive as he was violent, just like Zeus.

"Smells like sex in here, man," Herk said.

My spine stiffened.

Damn.

"You got something to say about that?" Zeus asked in his *don't-fuck-with-me* voice.

I winced and looked over at Odin, who leaned in the corner, watching.

Why wasn't Odin worried?

It would be a rough fight, Zeus v. Herk. Zeus had extensive military training, but Herk had that unpredictability thing going. No doubt a fight between them would end with broken bones, wrecked teeth, ruptured organs.

Possibly even a visit to the hospital.

"I'm saying it smells like sex," Herk growled.

I held my breath.

"You got a problem with that?" Zeus growled.

They seemed to be squaring off.

Odin snorted. "You want *fucking-g* customer service, you should go to Starbucks."

I sucked in a breath.

Herk shot a steely glance at Odin. "What's that?"

"That's our *fucking-g* tagline." Odin grinned his beautiful, dangerous grin. "What do you think?"

Herk went still for just a moment, then he burst out laughing in great booming bellows.

He turned back to Zeus and clapped a hand on his shoulder. "I'm not telling you for me, man, I'm telling you for other customers. Normal customers." This was actually meaningful, a kind of declaration. It was Herk casting in as one of us. "I know what you got here," he added, nodding at me respectfully.

I nodded back and I went around to take a seat at my desk and opened up my laptop, giving them attention privacy. If they needed real privacy, they could go into Zeus's office, but they weren't doing that. I was glad they weren't.

"So what's up?" Zeus asked. "And anything you say here is cone of silence, of course," he added. "You can trust Odin. You can trust Ice."

"Yeah, I know you'll keep it cool." Herk went to the window and looked out over the street.

I used the opportunity to pull out the fabulous P.I. notepad that I'd bought online. It had a leather cover and a tiny embossed fleur-de-lis in the upper corner.

"You know I was set to marry Maria, right?"

Zeus nodded. "Got yourself a princess."

I flicked my gaze to Odin, realizing suddenly that they were talking about Maria Galvano, who was Don Galvano's daughter… and that merely by standing in this room with these guys, I was probably two degrees of separation from the FBI's entire twenty-most-wanted list. Aside from the stray chop-em-up psycho killer type.

We drew the line at associating with chop-em-up psycho killer types, even as Facebook friends.

"Princess, yeah. It's been a big fucking problem—you know how those mafiosos wanna see their daughters with Italian boys. Her father? Big fucking problem, man." He shook his head. "It's taken me two fucking years to warm old Galvano to the idea of me and his girl. Maria says she doesn't care. She's always going on, *let my fucking family disown me, I don't give a shit.* But I give a shit because I know how that works. You don't make your woman choose between her family and you. Especially once you start having kids, right? You want to have your people around you, to make a proper home, right? Death, birth, holidays, you need your people around you—that's what it's all about. And kids need grandparents and all that. Anyway, finally after two years I'm showing up enough with the old man that he's giving me some respect."

I nodded. It was very sweet.

"Last month I asked for Maria's hand the old-fashioned way. You know mafiosos. Never met a tradition they don't wanna get in bed with. I get the old man after dinner. Break out a nice old bottle of scotch. I tell him I'm gonna ask her. The old man says yes, so we're good. Everyone's good. We set the date for a big Catholic wedding. My folks are Catholic, too, so that's something we all have in common."

"Congratulations," Odin said.

"Not yet," Herk said. "Because somebody went and fucked me —really messed everything up."

We waited patiently while Herk ran his tongue over his teeth in a brooding, threatening way. "Old man has this beloved vintage Corvette. If you ask me, it's an old guy's car that's designed to say, *Look at me, I'm not an old guy.* The last thing I'd ever want is to drive in that thing, but in front of the Don, I always act like his car's the shit. Man's car. Form of respect."

"Can't criticize a man's car," Zeus said.

"Not a car like that," Odin said.

I stifled a smile because we were all thinking *penis* of course.

Herk leaned back on the wall. He'd been avoiding the chairs, as were my guys. None of them wanted to sit. None wanted the height disadvantage.

I settled down in my comfy chair and flung my feet up on the desk, just because I could.

Dudes.

I sighed contentedly and made a mental note to get a few stools to allow the many alphaholes who might come through here to sit without losing their height advantage. Including my own personal alphaholes.

Odin gave me a sly look. I gave him a superior smile.

Herk went on with his story. "So Maria's parents and some of their capos are over in the old country for a month. Sicily, mostly.

Their place is down to skeleton staff. Maria and I went over a few times to use the tennis court, but that's it."

"You guys play tennis together?" Zeus asked.

Herk nodded. "Tennis is a sport you can play with a girl, and you can play it your whole life long. You want to be thinking ahead on these things. Family, kids, holidays, togetherness, growing old together."

I loved how sentimental Herk was. I hoped we could help him.

Partly it was because I felt sad about the sisters I'd left behind. I'd had to fake my own death last year—it was the only way I could protect them; my bank robbers' powerful enemies became my powerful enemies, but there wasn't anything I wouldn't've given to see them again, hug them. To decorate the Christmas tree—why had I always seen it as such a chore? Or even spend a night huddled in the lambing barn together with a thermos of coffee. Or curled up on the couch with popcorn. I missed lying awake at night in the rural stillness, when a strange noise out in the darkness just meant raccoons were probably getting into the garbage.

I wanted Herk and Maria to have that. Not the raccoons, but the picturesque future.

Herk had gotten to the important part of his story by the time I tuned back in: Don Galvano and his crew had arrived back from Italy a week ago only to find the precious Corvette missing. Stolen.

"Was he recording?" Odin asked.

"He was *recording*," Herk said, doing air quotes.

Zeus and Odin nodded, like, oh, of course, *he was "recording."*

I found myself wishing Thor were there so that he could explain what that meant. As they talked on, I started feeling a little out of my depth. I'd always been good at solving puzzles, and I'd imagined I'd make a good detective, but it was right around this moment that I realized how really useless I was.

I might've made a good detective for normal people, but there was a baseline of normal in the criminal set that I didn't understand, even after a year within it, like what it meant to be *air-quotes-recording*.

It was such a fabulous idea, to be detectives for people who had too much to hide to go to the cops, and I really did want to be helpful, to be part of it, but apparently I'd do just as well breaking out a magnifying glass and Sherlock Holmes hat and solving pressing mysteries among the billy goat community.

Herk went on to recount how he offered to put out the word and help the old man find his car. "Between me and the Don, we have our beaks dipped in most of the chop shops south of Malibu," Herk added, creating a truly strange mental image.

I bit my lip.

When I looked up, Odin was staring at me knowingly. I forced myself to look away, to look like I was concentrating really hard on Herk's tale.

A week later, apparently, the cops found Don Galvano's amazing vintage Corvette smashed up near Crenshaw—right near one of Herk's corners, which naturally cast suspicion on Herk.

Then they got traffic surveillance showing a man with long dark hair driving the thing east out of Santa Monica toward Herk's turf. There was a blob on his arm that could've been Herk's tattoo. They used the data from the traffic cams to determine the route. Galvano then pulled surveillance footage from his businesses on the route. He got a direct and very distinct hit: the Corvette idling at a red light in front of one of his laundromats.

"High-definition shit," Herk said. "Other guys have my hair, but nobody has my tattoo. You ever see it?"

Zeus had, but Odin and I hadn't.

Herk pulled off his jacket and dress shirt and rolled up the sleeve of his white T-shirt to reveal a magnificent and massive fire-bird tattoo, wild with reds, yellows, oranges, and fury. The thing took up most of his upper arm, bright and gorgeous across his skin.

Odin whistled. "That's some distinctive work."

"Oh, it's distinctive," Herk said. "Nobody else has this. Which means somebody took a photo of it and re-created it and wore a wig. Did an amazing job of framing me."

"You got an alibi?" Zeus asked.

Herk shook his head. "I was staking out a job with one of my guys at the time. Does me no good."

"Your guy can't tell Galvano that?" I asked.

"My guys would die for me," Herk grumbled. "You think they wouldn't lie for me? The old man knows it."

"Don Galvano has cops on the payroll," Zeus said. "Did they lift any prints?"

"Nah. Driver was wearing gloves in the shots, anyway," Herk said, putting his outfit back to rights.

"So somebody was trying to ruin your relationship," I said.

"Somebody *did* ruin it. Presented with fucking photographic evidence that makes it look like I took a joyride in her dad's Corvette? Making me look like I crashed it and lied? She wants to believe me, she mostly believes me, but the doubt is there, man. I see it in her eyes, and it's killing everything about us. I vowed to her I'd prove it wasn't me. I thought I had time…" His nostrils expanded as he huffed out a breath. He strode over to the window. "Now I find out her fucking dad's sending her for two years to Oxford—only way he'll pay for her college is if she goes."

"Oh, no," I whispered, getting into it.

"She gets on that plane, and we're done. She says not. But I know it. Don Galvano knows it."

I nodded. "The doubt is bad. And then being sent overseas…"

"I'm losing her, man. She's my life. " His voice cracked. It was wild to see this big, tough man brought so thoroughly to his knees. He loved her. "I just need to stop her from leaving. I need to show her and her father it wasn't me."

"You got a sense of who'd do this?" Odin asked. "You know who would frame you?"

"That's what I'm coming to you for," Herk said. "I'm hiring you to get me a name. Because me and whoever did this..." He fixed Zeus with a hard look, then he turned it on Odin, then on me, and the air went dead cold— "me and whoever this is, we've got issues."

Issues.

There were a lot of places I didn't want to be just then— prison. Hell. Strapped into the chair of an insane dentist. Being on the other end of those *issues* with Herk Washington would definitely rank right up there.

"But you have a guess, a suspicion, enemies that spring to mind," Odin said, moving around to lean back on the desk, forming a triangle with Zeus and me. I got the feeling that even the way my guys configured their bodies was carefully calibrated to show that they were enclosing Herk with their strength, but not threatening him.

Watching my guys use their professional acumen was always a thing of beauty. I'd seen it before, when I had been the target of a stalker, and now here it was again.

It gave me chills. Good chills.

"Lotta guys it could be," Herk said.

Odin eyed him, head tilted in a way that seemed to say, *let's consider this together.* "Five? Ten? How many?"

"Guys who'd have it out for me?"

"Yeah, who out there would want to fuck you up in this particular way?" Zeus asked. "The crime itself tells us a lot. It allows us to rule out everybody who wants to kill you. What does that leave in? Three groups of people. In the first group you got those who have it out for you, but not bad enough to kill you—they just want to make you miserable." Zeus held up two fingers now. "Second group—people who have their reasons for not wanting you to get close to Don Galvano, which could include the Don's own guys. Third group: people angling to break you and Maria up for reasons of jealousy or otherwise."

Odin handed him a pad of legal paper. "Make a list. Anyone in those three groups."

Herk started writing.

Odin went on to quiz Herk on his knowledge of Don Galvano's operations. Did he know the coin laundromat was there? How well known was it that he had a coin laundromat there? The whole line of questioning seemed odd. Personally, I was wondering why Galvano had a coin laundromat at all, or why that laundromat would have a camera pointed to the traffic in front of it...but then I realized I probably didn't want to know.

"We'll need to see all the footage," Odin said. "Who has it?"

"Galvano."

"What's your status with him?" Zeus asked. "Does he know you're having this looked into? You think he'll let us have copies?"

"I don't know. He's pissed. And more secretive than ever, due to...new *organizational realities.*"

My guys nodded, like that was all really clear.

Herk scribbled down a few more names and looked up. "Fuck, man, you wouldn't catch me dead driving a Corvette. Please. But can I say that? No." He scribbled down another name. "Whoever did this, they're gonna wish they killed me." He tapped his pen on the pad. "All eight James brothers are pissed at me, but not enough to kill me. Do I need to name them separately?"

Odin looked over his shoulder. "Just write James brothers. What's your beef with them?"

"Disputed territory shit. They wouldn't like the idea of the alliance, my people with Galvano in the background."

Odin asked, "Who's Nico Piazolla?"

"Maria's old boyfriend. He was pissed when we started things up. I could see him behind this. And my old corner guy Henry— right here—he did a two-year bid off beating a guy on one of my corners. I hear he thinks I didn't do enough witness intimidation on his behalf. I could see him behind this."

Herk went on and on. The list was like twenty names long—

more if you considered that some of the names were groups, like the James Gang, as I preferred to call them.

"That's a lot of enemies," Zeus said.

"Fuck it," Herk said. "Shows you're doing something right as far as I'm concerned."

"We'll analyze that footage. That's where we start," Odin said.

"You sure you need the footage?" Herk asked.

"It's the only known footage of the person impersonating you—in high definition," Zeus said. "We definitely need it."

"So what if I say I don't think he'd give up the footage? Is that a deal breaker?"

"You *fucking-g* insult us, Herk," Odin said. "A thing we need is behind lock and key." Odin turned to Zeus. "Zeus, a thing we want and need is behind lock and key. What do we do about that? How will we ever get it?"

"Hmm," Zeus said. "If only we had skills in that area."

"Hold on—fuck—" Herk said. "I don't want you robbing him."

"You want your mystery solved or not?" Odin asked. "You hire the badass bank robbers, you get the badass bank robbers."

"I'm not sending three guys with AKs to do a violent takeover of the Don's house. I'm in deep enough shit with him here."

"Now you're being insulting," Zeus said. "Violent takeovers aren't our only move. It's just the one that gets on the news the most."

"*Fucking-g* news is so sensationalized," Odin said. "Such bullshit."

"I don't want you breaking in quietly either," Herk growled. "The whole point is to repair our relationship. Jesus."

Thor walked in just then, still in his scrub pants, blond hair tied back in a short ponytail. He slung his satchel off his shoulder and onto the desk. "You guys started without me?" He headed to Herk, hand outstretched. "How's it going, man?"

"Thor." Herk took his hand and they shook.

Thor smiled. "Alexander Hamilton, huh?"

Herk snorted. "That's what you get for asking. Thanks again for Ethan."

"He using that shot arm okay?"

"Good as new," Herk said. I realized that Thor must have treated one of Herk's guys. Thor sometimes had gunshot victims coming his way.

Zeus turned to Herk. "We need that footage from the Don. One way or another."

Herk frowned, rocking slightly. Not quite a nod. "Fine. I'll tell him you're coming. You're going to have to be cool with him, though. Repairing bridges here. Not burning them."

Zeus nodded. "Don't worry, we know how to talk to this guy. Go ahead and give him a call. Tell him we're coming. He probably has his car out for work somewhere, and we need to get to it before the forensic evidence gets fucked up. Which it already will be, but we can maybe get something."

Zeus led him into the back office.

"What'd I miss?" Thor asked, bending over to kiss me.

There was a glint in Odin's eyes. "Isis wants us to fuck her in front of a stranger."

"Stop it!" I said. "Don't talk about that anymore. It flips Zeus out too much."

"Ooh, Ice." Thor went over to where my legs still rested atop the desk and laid a hand on one bare calf. "What about Herk?"

"Is Herk short for Hercules?"

"Probaby. You want us to fuck you in front of him?" Thor asked.

"Are you insane?" I exclaimed. "He's a client. And a dangerous drug lord!"

Odin snorted and came around to my other side. "It would take a lot more than a dangerous drug lord to keep us from getting it up for you, goddess."

"You have to stop this whole watching thing. Zeus hates it."

"Zeus is being *fucking-g* inflexible," Odin said. "It's not as if we're inviting another man to fuck you."

"Zeus isn't into it?" Thor seemed surprised by this.

"He's forbidden it."

Thor straightened. "What the fuck?"

"You have to respect that," I said.

"Yeah, well, Zeus didn't want you in the gang in the first place," Thor said. "Maybe he needs a little prodding."

"He's serious," I said.

"What if we tied Herk up?" Odin suggested. "He thinks you're hot. And he would be watching, wishing it was him."

"He's our first client," I said. "We can't tie him up and have sex in front of him. That's not how a private investigation firm is supposed to work. Plus he loves Maria."

Thor pulled the elastic band from his ponytail and shook out his hair, looking every inch the hot Swedish soccer player. Or maybe tennis player. Not a bad dilemma to have. "We can do anything we want. That's one of the fringe benefits of being outlaws."

"What do you say, goddess?" Odin said.

"Let me think about this a sec. Do I want you to tie Herk up and fuck me in front of him, thereby losing our first client and angering Zeus, not to mention Herk himself? Um..." I put my finger prettily to my cheek. "*NO!*"

"Not your type," Odin said. "That's the problem, isn't it?" He ran his finger up the inner part of my thigh, creating an invisible line of sensation that got me a little hot.

Thor grinned. "You have a type for watching? This is getting interesting."

"No," I said.

"Yes she does," Odin said.

I sniffed.

"I bet you'd like him tied up," Odin said, trailing his finger back down toward my knee. My mouth went dry—he always knew exactly how to touch me. "Whoever watches, you'd want him tied up. Reluctant. Chafing at his restraints. Right?"

A warm, delicious feeling bloomed in my belly. "Subject closed."

"Yes or no?" Odin said, sliding his finger back up again, up under my skirt this time.

I shoved back, took my legs off the desk, and stood to face him, planting a finger in the middle of his chest. "A, Herk is right in the other room, so shut it. And B, a kink is only fun if all parties involved are into it."

"Let's not get extreme, goddess," Odin said.

Thor smirked.

Herk and Zeus came back out just then. I shot Odin and Thor warning looks as Zeus and Herk shook hands.

Zeus had been getting more intense and possessive lately—couldn't they see that? It was wrong to push him and goad him.

Zeus turned to us once Herk was out the door. "You up to speed, Thor?"

Thor smiled. "Certainly am."

"Come on," Zeus said. "Don Galvano's expecting us in an hour."

Chapter Four

Don Galvano presided over his old-school mafia family from a deco-style mansion in the Palisades. Zeus pulled our vehicle *du jour*, a black Range Rover, up to ornate white gates.

"Pearly," I said.

Odin smirked.

I was sitting sandwiched between Odin and Zeus up front. Thor was in back tapping and clicking his phone.

"It's good you're here, goddess," Odin said. "It will more social, less like gangster shit."

"Not to mention you promised I'm an equal player in this," I reminded them all. "Except for instances of clear and present danger."

It was a promise they might be regretting, but they'd made it, and I didn't intend to let them forget.

A man came out of a little white watchman box and ambled up to the driver's side window.

Zeus told him we were friends of Herk's, and that the Don was expecting us. The guy nodded and instructed us to wait. Then he went back into his wee hut.

"Nice place. What's Galvano into?" I asked.

"These days he's mostly extortion and gambling with some extended interests in Vegas," Zeus said. "A little bit of high-end flesh."

"Oh, high-end flesh," I said. "That's classy."

Quick as a flash, Zeus had me on his lap, face right close to mine. "You got something to say about my choice of terminology?"

"Sure do," I snorted, pulse racing.

"Do I need to bend you over my knee?"

Sure might, I thought.

"Oh, Isis," Odin said sadly, snaking a hand around my belly.

Zeus took my lips in a furiously dominating kiss as the gate opened. He broke off the kiss but kept hold of me on his lap as he drove through. We parked at the end of a line of shiny cars, most of them big and black.

I heard a zipper sound in the back. *Here?*

But it was Thor's satchel.

We got out. Zeus threw on a sport jacket and sunglasses. With his short brown hair and muscular grace, he had the look of a billionaire Navy SEAL, which I can tell you was not a bad look at all.

Odin was in black—basic black button-down hanging open over a black T-shirt. Black jeans. Black hair. Black lush eyelashes. Black five o'clock shadow. Black smarty-pants eyeglasses, his usual delectability. Poor Odin always tried so hard to tone down his beautiful male model looks and go for a gruff badass appearance, and it never worked. He could glue a dead tarantula to his nose, and even then, people would be like, *why does that super-hot guy have a dead tarantula glued to his nose?*

Thor took my arm as we walked up the steps. He was Mr. Casual, still in his scrub pants and corduroy shirt.

I always felt so proud, going places with my hot and wonderful guys. And right there I decided the watching thing was stupid. Yeah, I liked thrills, but what more did I need than these three awesome men? I was the luckiest woman on the planet.

Zeus rang the doorbell. I smoothed my skirt and grabbed a mint from my purse. Thor put out his hand so I gave him one, then Zeus and Odin wanted mints, too. Sometimes they were like kids, really.

The door was opened by a giant man with zero body fat, a large weaponry bulge under his jacket, and a shaved head to complete the extra-fierce look. "You're Herk's people?" he asked.

"Yup. Here to see the Don."

The guy nodded and led us through one room and another, each more lavishly bedecked than the last.

We finally arrived in the study where we found the Don, a large man with a big belly, a bald dome of a head, and an expression like he just ate a lemon.

His study was very classic, lined with bookcases that were stuffed with dusty-looking hardcover books. The furniture was all dark wood and leather, and there was even a globe on a stand.

And it was all super-masculine. Even the globe was black—none of that pastel shit for the mafia don! The man liked a fucking black globe!

"Don Galvano." Zeus held out his hand. "Thanks for agreeing to meet with us. And Herk really appreciates it, too."

"Yeah, I heard you're P.I.s now," the Don said. "I had to see this for myself. The three of you, now the four, you got more heat on you than I ever did." He gestured back and forth, sweeping us all into his sentence. "What the fuck are you doing with the P.I. shit?"

"We're investigating this matter with Herk..."

"No, no, no, I don't give a shit about that. That's not why I agreed to meet you. I just gotta ask you what you're doing. Considering the kind of heat you have on you, I mean..." he gestured again. "The kind of heat I have on me, I can pull outta that heat of in a court of law. I'm a *legitimate businessman.*"

Of course he didn't bother with air quotes for *legitimate busi-nessman*. Those air quotes were assumed, I guess, and it would be uncool to use them, in the same way it would be dorky if my bank robbers put air quotes around the phrase *make a withdrawal* when they talked about knocking over a bank. The underworld version of suspenders and flood pants.

"But your kind of heat," he continued. "I mean, if your people catch up with you, that's not going to be resolved in a court of law. That shit is going to be resolved in the belly of a tanker, if you catch my meaning. Why would you risk these kinds of investigations?"

"Never mind about us," Odin said.

Practically right at the same time, Zeus said, "We'll worry about our own safety."

"No, wait," I said. "Investigating a crime is way safer than a bank robbery."

Galvano snorted. "Think it through."

"Can we get back to business?" Odin said. "We're here on Herk's behalf."

"No, I want to hear what the Don has to say," I said.

"Who can hurt you?" the Don asked.

I was thinking the police, but mostly ZOX, the covert agency Zeus and Odin were once in. They were eternally after us. Especially the agent assigned to our case, Agent Denko.

"The feds, right?" the Don said.

"They can only hurt us if they can find us," I say.

The Don raised his brows.

Riiiiight. Somebody could help ZOX find us.

"Nobody's going to *fuck with* us," Odin said.

"Could I hurt you?" the Don asked.

"You wouldn't," Zeus said.

"Give me a reason to hurt you, I might. When you were only hitting banks, nobody in our community had a problem with you.

I'd go as far as to say you had empathy and respect from every corner, poking a stick into the man's eye like you do."

I nodded, knowing it was true. Nothing says *fuck you* to the man like a big, loud takeover-style bank robbery in broad daylight.

"Everybody loves seeing you guys ripping off banks. But let's pretend for a moment that asshole Herk isn't the one who crashed my car. I know it was him, but let's pretend it wasn't. That means somebody else did it. That means some guy out there knows you're taking all your skills you developed over all those years of doing whatever covert shit you were doing and you're pointing all those skills at him. You're coming for him. Suddenly, you got yourself an enemy inside the community, and you don't know who the fuck he is. But he knows who you are."

"Oh my god," I said. I hadn't thought of that.

Zeus shook his head. "It's fine, Ice."

Odin glowered.

"What better way to save themselves than drop a dime to the feds? Let 'em know the God Pack is back in L.A. and even where you'd be."

"Nobody would do that, goddess," Thor said softly, "because they know they'd die."

"You so sure about that?" Galvano asked. "Nobody thinks they're going to get caught—not even by you. You're successful bank takeover guys. Why hang out a fucking shingle like this when you have all the money in the world?"

"Because we are awesome investigators who spit in the faces of our enemies," Odin said.

"And nobody tells us what to do or stops us from helping our friends," Thor added. "We believe Herk, and we're going to prove he's innocent."

And I believed that for Thor and Odin, these were the reasons. Defiance. Excellence. Righting wrongs.

But for Zeus, it was something more.

I turned to him and waited for him to explain why it was so important to him to start the agency, even in the face of danger.

"A man does what he does," Zeus answered simply.

A man does what he does?

The Don held up his hand, sensing this was all he'd get. "Okay. Fine."

But it wasn't enough for me, and I couldn't help but think about what the Gigis, a gang of female jewel thieves, had said in the bathroom one time—that my guys were on a death sprint that would end with them crashing and burning.

"Now can we get to Herk's matter here?" Zeus said.

"Herk? The piece of shit who took my car for a joyride and won't own up to it?" Don Galvano waved the air, waving an imaginary Herk aside.

I felt so angry on Herk's behalf. I knew he wouldn't have come to us if he wasn't innocent.

"It's only for Maria's sake he's not lying in a ditch with his balls cut off," the Don said.

Inwardly I winced.

Zeus said, "We'd love to take a look at that footage you have."

"So you can torque up some excuse why it's not him? The footage shows him clear as day driving my car. He thought he could take it for a joyride while we were across the pond, and he wouldn't fess up once he wrecked it."

"You think your future son-in-law would hire somebody as awesome as us if he did it?"

"Maybe he's hired you to effect his cover-up," the Don said. "To twist around the scenario—"

"We don't do cover-ups," Zeus growled, moving toward Galvano. "And if you think just because Herk's paying us that we're his bitches, you're wrong. And if you think cover-ups are our business, we've got a major fucking problem between us."

Odin slapped his hand onto Zeus's shoulder, urging restraint, but he looked like he wanted to kill the Don himself. "We were trained as *fucking-g* investigators. We will not be manipulated. We will not be bought."

I held my breath as Thor echoed them. My guys had first met when Odin had been sent to kill Thor, who'd been working as a doctor with an aid organization and had reported atrocities. When Odin had arrived and learned the truth, he'd decided to protect Thor. The not-supposed-to-exist agency ZOX had then sent their very, very best weapon—Zeus—out to kill them both, but Zeus, too, turned against ZOX. The three of them made a lot of trouble bringing the truth to light and earned targets on their backs forever.

Thus began their lives as fugitives. High-performance outlaws.

Don Galvano shrugged. "I'm not playing Herk's game."

Zeus got a little bit in his face. "Are you suggesting we can't get to the truth or won't get to the truth?"

"Hold on." I put a hand on Zeus's arm. "Let me ask you, Mr. Galvano, where is Maria on all this?"

"She wants to believe that scumbag, but she saw the tapes," the Don said. "It'll be good for Maria to get out of here."

"And what if it wasn't Herk?" I asked him. "You're trying to help Maria by sending her out of the country, but what if she finds out it wasn't Herk, but it's too late? And what if she finds out you blocked Herk's one chance to clear his name? Maybe you don't want to cooperate with us for Herk's sake, and I understand that. But don't you want to be sure of your facts for Maria's sake?"

The Don sniffed, unconvinced, but I thought I might be getting through.

I looked down at my fingernails, long and lovely and pink. "What do you have to lose? If we find out it really was him, well, all the better."

"And if it's not him," Odin said, "you get to put somebody else in the ditch with their balls cut off—"

"An extremely unpleasant way to go," Thor interjected.

Odin continued, "Imagine if somebody out there is fucking with you. Laughing at you. Wouldn't you want to know?"

The Don was silent for a while. "You think there's any kind of chance it wasn't Herk?"

"We got an open mind and badass skills," Zeus said. "It's just some footage, man."

The Don frowned. "What kind of confidentiality can I expect in terms of telling you where this camera is placed?"

Zeus merely tilted his head, fixing the Don with a level stare.

The Don looked thoughtful. He wandered over to his badass black globe and gave it a spin, then another. Then he stepped out of the room and into the hallway to speak in hushed tones with the guy who'd let us in—the butler, or whatever you'd call a butler-bodyguard combination, which probably shouldn't be but-guard.

Odin came around and put his hands on my shoulders. "What do you think about him, Ice?"

"Stubborn," I said, "but he cares about his daughter."

"No, is he your *type*?" Odin clarified. "To watch?"

I spun around. "Are you out of your mind?"

Zeus got up into Odin's face. "Isis doesn't want a watcher."

"If that's what you think," Odin growled, "then you haven't been paying attention."

Zeus took hold of Odin's shirt. "We don't share her."

Thor said, "It's not sharing to have an audience. It's about fulfilling Isis's fantasy."

Zeus cast a wild glance at Thor, still holding Odin by the shirt. "You're on his side?"

Thor put up his hands. "I'm on the side of maximizing Isis's pleasure."

"This fighting isn't maximizing my pleasure," I whispered loudly.

Zeus kept his hands on Odin.

Odin looked wild and energized, and there was a mad gleam in his eyes.

"You guys, come on!"

"She has a type for watching," Odin said. "Ask her."

"We don't share Isis," Zeus said. "No watchers."

Odin's eyes glittered. "Is that a new rule?"

Zeus frowned and yanked him harder.

My heart pounded. "Stop it!"

"Is it true? You have a type for watching, Ice?" Zeus asked, not taking his eyes from Odin.

"Fuck you both! My type is you guys!" I tried to pull them apart. No go.

"Yes or no," Odin said. "Tell him. You have a type for watching. Is it this guy? An in-charge operator?"

"We're not making a mafia don watch us have sex," I said. "Not that we could."

"I can make anybody do anything." Odin's threatening tone chilled me. It was sometimes easy to forget how really dangerous these guys were.

It was probably bad that that turned me on a little bit.

I looked over at Thor, who seemed amused. Of course. He loved chaos.

"All of you can fuck off," I said. "Seriously. Fuck off."

Don Galvano was suddenly back in the room. "Everything alright?"

Odin smiled as Zeus released him. "Office politics," he said.

The Don went around the desk, opened a laptop, and shoved a thumbdrive into the slot. "Here's the footage. This is your copy. Personalized."

I assumed there was some significance to that personalized comment. Probably a threat in there, like he'd be able to know if we shared it.

"Here, take a look at Herk in my 'vette," the Don said. "It's at 50:41."

We gathered around the back of the desk and watched the

streetscape on the screen. Cars whizzed by, back and forth. Now and then they rolled to a stop.

"Red light," Don Galvano said. "Your boy's up next."

The light changed and the cars sailed by once again. A white Corvette was the first to stop at the next red light. I bit my lip. Herk. The shot wasn't great, even for high definition, but it was clearly him. The long hair. The tattoo. Don Galvano paused the clip and selected the area for zooming in. The video got pixelated close up. But wow, it was damning.

"Hmm," Odin said.

"Definitive enough for you?" the Don said. "You gonna tell me somebody wore a wig and went through that kind of trouble to get that tattoo painted on his arm? And for what? If Herk's got an enemy who'll go through that amount of trouble, this isn't what they're going to do."

"This is helpful," Odin said.

The Don wasn't satisfied. "You see what I'm talking about?"

"We see that it's convincing," Zeus said.

The Don rolled his eyes.

"Do a lot of people know about this camera?"

"Not a lot. Not at all."

"Herk? Maria?"

He shook his head.

"How many of these cameras do you have between here and there?" Odin asked.

"I'm going to tell you *that* now?" The Don barked—it wasn't really even a laugh.

"Put it this way," Zeus said, standing. "If we were to hop in a car and drive aimlessly around the surface streets for an hour, how likely are we to pass one of these babies? Not asking where, just level of coverage."

"On a light traffic day," Thor added.

"An hour? Mmm..." The Don pondered this.

"How about ninety minutes?" Zeus said after a while.

"Ninety, I'd imagine you'd pass one. An hour, you're getting lucky."

"So it's not like they're all over the place," Zeus said.

"No."

"Where's the car now?" Zeus asked.

The Don gave us the address of a garage just off Aviation Boulevard. "The driver wore gloves. You won't get shit, and I'm sure the repairs are underway by now."

"We'd like to visit the thing in any case," Odin said.

"Fine," the Don said. "And if you want to talk again, don't come to my home. Nothing personal. You know."

Just the heat.

We thanked him and left.

"This watching bullshit stops here," Zeus growled once we got out to the SUV. He unlocked the door and got into the driver's seat.

"If you're not into it, you don't have to participate," Odin said, sliding into the passenger side.

Thor and I climbed into the back.

Zeus just sat there, not pulling out, not even putting the key into the ignition.

"What? Let's go," Odin said.

"No watchers when I'm not around, either," Zeus said finally.

The air seemed to go out of the car.

"What's that?" Thor said.

"You heard me," Zeus said.

"You can't make a pronouncement like that," Odin said.

"And do you mean public sex when there's a danger of a watcher?" Thor clarified. "Or what about a gloryhole—"

"Wait, what?" I said. "When did a gloryhole come into this?"

"I don't want you guys to fuck in front of anyone when I'm not around," Zeus said. "What part of that don't you understand? I don't want you guys. To *fuck* in front of *anyone*. When I'm not *around*." He started up the engine.

"I don't know how much I like this," Odin said.

"Wasn't designed for your pleasure," Zeus said.

We drove out the gates in silence. This was a major thing. A shift in something deep underground.

We rode to the main thoroughfare in silence.

Zeus was the leader in fighting situations. And he was the one who vetoed me joining the gang, and then the one who finally let me in. But making a rule like this?

Thor focused on his phone. He had to check it a lot, due to his clinic, but he liked to look at it when he wanted to tune things out. That's what he was doing now. Odin just glittered, staring straight ahead, a little bit too energized by the fight.

I felt worried for our foursome. Was this how couples broke up? From people wanting different things? Having four people left even more room for differences than being just two. My heart began to pound as I tried not to think about the Beatles and pretty much every other rock band in history.

"I believe in us," I said. "I believe in our ability to work out anything together."

Odin said nothing.

"Come here." Thor pulled me to him, and I leaned on him, enjoying his arms around me. "Don't worry, goddess," he whispered, still focused on his phone.

I nestled into him, but the tension in the truck was killer.

"What does the number of cameras have to do with anything? Why does it matter if you drive around for one hour or five hours before you hit one of his cameras?"

Odin said, "If the Don has establishments with sophisticated cameras on every street, that's one thing. But if the Don only has a few cameras out there, what are the chances the culprit would drive past one that's on a street corner just in time to be stopped at a traffic light so that the camera can get a good long shot? Fewer cameras would suggest the imposter knew about this camera. Assuming it's an imposter."

"You think it could be Herk?" I asked.

"Got to keep an open mind on that." Odin twisted back around. "It was good what you said, Isis. The thing about Maria."

"Yeah," Zeus said. "You had the golden touch there."

"I think you would've gotten through to him eventually," I said.

"Don't know about that," Zeus said. "If you hadn't been there, we would've probably had to get it the hard way."

Chapter Five

THE AUTOMOTIVE GARAGE THE DON SENT US TO WAS A
hulking and slightly lopsided building on an endless strip of road
ruled by storage facilities, shitty chain restaurants, and scrub plants
growing through chain-link fences.

We parked next to a beater tow truck and headed for the door
that had *office* painted in crude red lettering above it. Thor carried
the case, which was a kit full of kits, basically.

Los Angeles was a town where appearances could be deceiving,
and this place was no exception; the inside was more like a posh
club for gents than body-shop reception area. It had leather seating, a nice rug, a wooden table with coffee services—pretty much
everything but a fireplace and a painting of an English hunting
scene.

A guy in a one-piece jumper came out, wiping his hands on a
rag. "You here for Mr. G's 'vette?"

Zeus nodded curtly.

The mechanic grunted and led us into the bowels of the place
where bright Crayola-colored tubes hung down from the ceilings
into shiny auto bays. The place was super-sophisticated, like Area
51 for really expensive cars.

Zeus took my hand as we walked through.

"Is this a chop shop, too?" I asked.

"What do you think?" Zeus asked, a little grumpy.

I pulled on his arm. "You okay?"

He looked down at me. "Not really."

"Are *we* okay?"

"You and me are," he said softly. "Always."

"I need all of us to be okay," I said.

He didn't reply.

We ended up at a repair bay on the far end staring at a white Corvette sitting atop a fat silver pole, its nose completely smashed. The Don's white Corvette.

Zeus let go of my hand. My guys walked all around the car, inspecting it.

"What's your impression?" Odin said to the guy.

"That Herk's one stupid motherfucker, that's what. He's lucky he still has his balls."

"No, of the damage," Odin said. "When you look at this damage, what comes to mind?"

He shrugs. "Shitty motherfucking driver."

They lowered the car and discussed it some more. The mechanic narrated his view of the events, showing where the driver scraped up along the side of one highway support pillar, then bounced to a wall and maybe spun. He ran a finger along the scrapes. "Still a bit of grit in there." He went over to the corner of the station and returned with a crunched-up white piece, which would have been lots of pieces if it hadn't been for strands of fiberglass holding the parts together. "This quarter panel took it head-on."

"Anyone here see the scene of the accident?" Odin asked. "You all towed it out, right?"

"Is that important?"

Odin nodded.

The man texted somebody.

"Any other impressions?" Odin asked.

Silence.

Personally, I was burning to share how shocked I was that Corvettes were basically made of plastic this whole time, but I knew that probably wasn't what he was going for.

"Like if it seems deliberate?" Odin added.

The man screwed up his face. "Hard to tell. When somebody goes down the boneheaded path, scrapes up against a wall or some such, it gets worse before it gets better as they overcorrect and lose their shit."

An urban beardsman in greasy overalls wandered up. Odin and Zeus quizzed him about how the car was found, and the man described the scene. He believed the driver had hit a wall, then spun and smashed into a nearby vehicle, then hit the wall again.

They opened up the driver's side door, then. "Who all has been in here?" Zeus asked.

"Couple of cops," our guide said.

"What did they do?"

"Shined their light around under the seat and so on. I think they were looking for trash. Didn't come out with anything."

"Thanks," Zeus said. "Ice, get the location of the accident. We'll go over this interior."

Thor set the suitcase on the rubberized mat.

I pulled out my fancy P.I. notepad, and then I looked over and caught Zeus smiling at me, and I knew he'd asked me to get the location just so I'd have an excuse to use the fancy notepad.

The urban beardsman showed me the location on his smartphone. I took down the coordinates and nearby streets on my pad and had him send me the photos he'd taken.

When I turned back, my guys were working like a well-oiled machine. Odin was kneeling just outside the driver's seat, inspecting it with a magnifying glass while Zeus shone a powerful light over his shoulder. Thor trained another light on the seat from the passenger side. The inside was pretty fucked up. The whole dash had been pulled apart, presumably for the stereo, and the seats were cut up.

"Whoever this was really went to town," I said.

"I'm guessing the stereo and seats were cut out after, but it's something we'd want to confirm," Zeus said.

Odin requested a baggie. I went into the case and got one, and I even held it open for him. He made a motion like he was putting something in there with tweezers. "Close it up."

"You didn't put anything in!" I said. "Were you just miming?"

He gave me a stern look that went to my gut.

I smiled, and in a low voice I said, "It's like you're mimes."

"Oh dear," Zeus said, in his we-might-have-to-punish-you-now voice.

"My thoughts exactly," Odin said. "It was a *fucking-g* fiber."

I tipped my head back and forth with just a bit of attitude as my world righted on its axis, with Odin and Zeus collaborating in their stern corrections of me.

If I had to insult them and endure a wicked round of spanking to bring my guys back together, so be it. I would gladly make that sacrifice. I was selfless like that. A total Mother Teresa.

"Mmm," Odin said, doing his tweezer mime again. But when he lifted it to the light I could see it—a long dark hair.

"Shit," I said. "Herk's."

"Maybe." Odin lifted his hand into the air like he was calling for quiet, but then Zeus slapped a magnifying glass onto his palm and Odin took a look, then shot a significant glance at Zeus. "If Herk wore a wig."

"Synthetic?" I asked.

"Mm-hmm," Odin said.

I brought out another baggie to capture this new evidence. "The don's going to eat his hat."

Zeus twisted his lush, brutish lips the way he sometimes did when he was pondering. "We won't show him yet."

"But it's so obvious—I mean, there's a wig hair the length and color of Herk's."

"But we're still Herk's people in his eyes," Zeus said. "If we want to clear Herk, we've got to catch this culprit. We need motive and opportunity. We need this guy on his knees confessing to the Don."

"That's a high bar," I said. "You set a high bar."

"We certainly do, goddess," Odin said. "And this is what you call a sweet little *fucking-g* break."

"Except there are a zillion wig stores in Southern California, and that's not counting movie studio prop departments and Halloween pop-up stores," I reminded him.

"Oh, it'll be hard," Zeus said. "A real fuck of a thing."

Odin took a deep breath. "A fuck of a thing that we will accomplish with blinding *fucking-g* awesomeness. And then we will come down like a thousand sledgehammers."

Thor crossed his arms, beaming into the distance. "Gotcha, motherfucker."

And just then I realized I was seeing something I hadn't seen in a very long time: my guys up against impossible odds. It was making them pull together. It was making them happy.

I hadn't believed Zeus when he had claimed he was bored just robbing banks. Should I have believed him? And anyway, better this than trying to rob Fort Knox or something, right?

Chapter Six

WE WENT OUT FOR LUNCH AT A MEXICAN RESTAURANT because that's something that you do when you're in a relationship with rich, successful bank robbers—you eat out a lot.

Guys.

My sleuthing Romeos identified two avenues of inquiry—the first was people on Herk's list, and the second was wig stores, theaters, and studios. It was decided that Odin would update Herk and ask around about the guys on the list, getting addresses and impressions. Meanwhile, Thor and Zeus and I would run down the wig angle.

So we spent the rest of the afternoon running down places that sold Herk-style wigs—Thor took ten of them, and Zeus and I took twelve.

Just FYI, investigating a crime isn't as much like *Law & Order* as you might think. Or maybe you could say it's like the most boring episode of *Law & Order* you could ever imagine, where there's a long car ride and a lot of waiting around between each equally boring conversation, and the people don't give as many random personal details either, which kind of disappointed me.

But it was fun to see Zeus in action. He had a way of making himself come off as a cop without having to directly say he was a cop; he'd just walk in presuming authority. Not only was this an effective investigation technique, but Zeus all bossy and stern and authoritative definitely got me hot. At each store he showed a screen grab of the driver and asked whether they'd sold wigs like that in the past two months—that's the time frame they'd decided on.

We quickly learned that wig stores have two main suppliers, and that the wig we were interested in was the B-160 22-inch, possibly the 20-inch, which retailed for around $150. A few of them had sold that model, and some of them had the purchase information to turn over. A couple of them needed to do research and get back to us. A few were stubborn about it.

No matter what, Zeus wanted me to note it all down on my P.I. pad.

"It's kind of boring," I said.

"Sometimes boring is good," Zeus said.

"Not for Maria and Herk. We have to save them, and this isn't getting us anywhere."

"Not directly," Zeus said. "These stores probably won't give us anything because whoever bought the wig isn't going to be stupid enough to use a credit card, but if you follow enough avenues, something turns up. You can't see a needle in a haystack, it's true, but if you grab enough handfuls of hay, you might get poked."

I narrowed my eyes. "Did you steal that out of a Sherlock Holmes book?"

Zeus gave me the stern gaze I so loved and pulled me to him and kissed me. I was kind of in the mood for fucking in the car after so many hours of Zeus being stern and commanding out in public, but somebody was all business.

A woman at one of the places remembered a deeply tanned man paying cash for a B-160 22-inch, but she thought it was related to a play or movie. Zeus got a really pathetic description and thanked her.

He told me later he didn't think our pool was limited to dark-skinned guys. Skin tone could be faked for surveillance-quality camera, a street side camera, just like hair and tattoos.

We reached the area of the crash after dusk and parked next to a boarded-up, graffiti-splashed bar that was enclosed by a big-ass metal gate. We got out. Zeus took my hand, and we set off. "Up there," he said.

The place seemed deserted but probably wasn't. The moon was full, luckily, since most of the streetlights were out. Most of the buildings were enclosed by fences of different heights; many of the fences were topped by curled claws strung with barbed wire for an extra-menacing effect. The street ran into an unused section of train track; on the other side was a tall concrete wall with a fence along the top bleeding down dark streaks of rust. There were lumps around a trash fire in the distance. Homeless.

"You got your piece?" I asked.

"Won't need it," Zeus said. "Most people down here, they get a sense of who they can fuck with and who they can't fuck with. It gets in the blood. The stupid ones who don't know who not to fuck with get thinned out fast."

"I guess," I said.

He kicked a can and kept going.

"You okay?"

Silence.

I took his hand and squeezed, looking around for the spot the beardsman described. Somewhere nearby there should be a washing machine on its side next to a tire pile.

"You play tennis?" he asked.

The emotion in his voice told me he was thinking about what Herk had said, about a couple growing old together. Tennis being nice for that and all. "I don't play tennis," I said.

"Me neither," he said.

He pointed to a patch of broken glass, glittering in the moon-light. We skirted around it.

"We could take lessons," I said.

"I don't know. Showing up at a place every Tuesday afternoon or something in tennis clothes? Seems ill-advised."

"Okay, then, we could hire a pro—what about that?"

He sniffed like it was so ridiculous.

"What?" I said. "You always say there's nothing you can't do, nothing you can't have."

"There's plenty we can't have," he said.

"Like what? Figure it out and we'll make a withdrawal." I felt all smart for not putting air quotes around *withdrawal.*

Then Zeus asked, "Can we withdraw a regular life, Isis? Like what Herk is looking for? Can we withdraw walking down the aisle someday?"

My mouth went dry. My smart feeling evaporated.

"Can we withdraw you meeting all my old friends from high school, and them making stupid wedding speeches? And us dancing to some piece of shit band playing '90s music, but we don't care, because we're in love? Can you withdraw that?"

My heart pounded. What was he talking about here? Leaving the gang?

"Can you withdraw settling down in a little place with a white picket fence and starting our own family and having the neighbors over for barbeques and being on a first-name basis with the mailman? And learning tennis because we know we'll be together forever?"

I stared forward, trying to compose my expression, but I was snagging on the *walk down the aisle* bit. And a little on the *starting our own family* bit. Well, actually the whole thing. It turned to him, and softly I asked, "Is that what you dream of, Zeus?"

"I know that's the kind of life you were trying to get away from," he said. "You love thrills and being breathless. You like danger and things a little crazy. But sometimes a farm seems like a little bit of heaven to me."

I couldn't help but notice he hadn't answered my question. "Is that what you dream about? Leaving them? Having it be just us?"

"No! God no! I love our gang, baby. I would lay down my life to keep us together."

I nodded, relieved.

"But it fucks me up to think about a simple normal family and holidays and shit. I don't want you to think I don't love what we all have. It's just that you grow up with these stupid dreams—"

"They're not stupid. Dreams are never stupid."

"We can never have that life."

"Is it what you dream about?" I ask.

"Sometimes, maybe."

I squeezed his hand, feeling heartbroken. The things he was talking about couldn't happen on any level.

"Whatever," he sniffed. "I dream of being in a rock band, too. So there's that."

"Zeus—don't. Don't minimize it." I could feel how deeply his desire ran, the pain of knowing things he'd dreamt of could never happen. "Zeus—"

"What?" He pulled his hand from mine and twisted my hair in a finger. "What do you think about putting Odin on drums? I think Odin would be awesome on drums. Thor would be on bass. You could play tambourine."

"I love you," I said. "There's that."

He looked grimly ahead.

We were nearing the shadowy-looking figures gathered around the fire, which smelled faintly of burning rubber. Zeus nodded a greeting in their direction, and we continued on. I pulled out my phone and found the picture of the accident scene that the beardsman had sent me. We identified the washing machine and the graffiti on the sides.

Zeus took out his phone and illuminated a band of white along the wall. Then he went to the wrecked train tracks and did a three-sixty turn. The man was in full-on investigator mode, seeing everything, feeling everything with his big animal instincts.

I felt such love at that moment, and I hurt for him, too, for all of the pain in his words. Of course he would have dreams that didn't involve being a dangerous fugitive. I was really the only one of us four who'd chosen this life. My guys were so fabulous and uber-capable, it was easy to forget they hadn't chosen this.

He crouched at the base of a massive utility pole, sifting through a patch of broken glass. I went and stood near him, just to be by him.

"He came down here specifically to crash it and walk away unseen," Zeus said. "Because if you crash a Corvette on well-traveled streets, you have people around with phones. Five calls to 911 before you even get out." He stood up and pointed. "He hit the thing first to test his nerve. Then he spun around and hit the nose under that yellow tag. Probably jarred him a bit. He hits here a final time with less force."

He seemed so sad. I want to tell him not to give up, that he could have a picket fence, but it would be a lie. He could have all the money and dark glory he wanted. He could have a diamond as big as his fist if he got it in his head to take it, but never a picket fence. Never neighborhood barbeques. Never a friendly mailman. At least, not one that they wouldn't want to kill.

He walked the scene, lost in concentration. This was a little bit like what he must have done when he was in ZOX—catching culprits. Righting wrongs. Had he dreamed of getting out of the field one day to become a ZOX bureaucrat with a family in D.C. or something? I wanted very much to ask, but I hesitated to, now that he was focusing on the investigation.

"Come on." He took my hand, and we headed over to the group around the fire.

"Are you kidding?"

"What? They're the perfect witnesses."

We drew near to the group of mostly middle-aged men who looked more weary than scary. Zeus asked them about the car. None of them saw the accident, but two of them were in the area when it happened and had heard it. They told him the driver was gone when they got to the car, and they argued for a while about what time it had been—late, but before midnight seemed to be the final verdict. Zeus thanked the group and gave them five hundred bucks. "Get something nice for the group of you," he said.

"That was nice," I said, walking away with him.

"If I'd've thought of it I would've brought more," he said. "What the fuck do we care? We're rich bank robbers."

❧

That night the four of us sat around our mod strip-of-fire fireplace that night comparing notes and making a battle plan for the next day. We didn't even have sex—that was how consumed my guys were with the investigation. A crashed car whodunit was a zillion steps down from the kind of investigation Zeus and Odin had been trained for, but they threw themselves into it with passion.

Odin wanted us to talk to the ex-boyfriend Nico together. He'd heard from a few different people beyond Herk that Nico had gotten angry when Herk had hooked up with Maria. Odin wanted to get to him before he got wind of our investigation.

So the next day we showed up to his bright new condo building near Venice Beach with coffee and a bag of chocolate-covered donuts. The doorman tried to hold us up while he cleared our visit with Nico. My guys didn't like that; instead, Odin babysat him with his 9mm while Zeus and Thor and I went up.

Nico lived on the fifth floor, but we took the stairs up instead of the elevator for whatever crime and spy world calculus they liked to use.

"Nice building," I said. "What's Nico into?"

"He's connected with the Borellis. Middle management," Thor said.

"Does that mean he's killed people?"

"He would've had to by now," Thor said. "He'll need to do

more before he gets made."

"He won't get made," Zeus said. "Too impulsive. Not trustworthy. Nice, though."

"He's nice until he's not," Thor said. "Nico's uncle had a gunshot wound last fall, and Nico was a real asshole about my work. He apologized, but what the fuck."

"Are the Borellis friends with the Galvanos?"

"Sometimes," Thor said mysteriously.

Nico didn't answer when we knocked, so Zeus whipped out his phone. "People need to start answering their doors, man."

"Who in their right mind would answer an unknown knock?" I said. "If somebody knocks without texting first, you know it's either a psycho or a Jehovah's Witness."

"Or us," Zeus said.

Thor texted, informing him that we were outside the door with donuts and coffee.

"What the fuck," Nico said, pulling open his door. His hair was lopsided with last night's product. He had classic Italian looks, and really, I could see him passing for Latino in the dark—even more so with a little arm bronzing. Especially with the kind of picture Don Galvano's laundromat had picked up.

"We brought you breakfast," Thor said, "and a few questions."

"You just show up at ten in the morning?" Nico said.

Thor walked in with the stuff. "We have Boemer's Donuts, dude."

You didn't need to be an ex-covert agent to know that Nico's main domestic activity was gaming, what with the takeout containers and couch and TV setup. He had a fabulous view of the water.

"Hey man, this is Ice," Zeus said.

I nodded.

Nico nodded back at me. "You didn't come for breakfast."

"Is it okay for Odin to come up?" Zeus asked. "He's held up with your doorman."

Nico rolled his eyes and called down to instruct the doorman to let Odin come up, then set his phone aside. "You should've called," he grumbled.

Thor pulled a donut from the bag and handed it to me—to get the eating started, I guess. "You hear about Don Galvano's Corvette?"

Nico sniffed. "I heard about it."

"What'd you hear?" Zeus asked.

"That Herk went on a joyride and cracked it up."

"Herk said it wasn't him," Zeus said. "That somebody made it look like him."

"Well I'd say the same thing if I crashed Galvano's car. You don't want to be crashing the old don's car."

Zeus eyed him. "Did *you*? Did you crash it?"

Nico adjusted his sinewy neck in a *WTF, did I even hear that right?* way. "Are you fucking kidding me?"

I'd seen my guys pull this technique before—the weirdly blunt question.

"I'm not kidding you, I'm asking you," Zeus said.

"That's why you came over here?"

Odin walked in.

"Don't bother knocking, man," Nico said.

"Did you crash the car?" Zeus asked again.

Nico locked the door. "In what universe would I drive or crash that car? Fuck no. It's not even a cool car."

"Where were you Tuesday night between ten and midnight?" Zeus pressed.

"What are you, the cops of the underworld?"

"Yeah," Odin said. "We are the *fucking-g* cops of the under-world, my friend."

Zeus crossed his arms. "Just want to know if you got an alibi."

"Yeah, I got an alibi." He pointed at the coffees. "One of those for me?"

"Yup."

Nico pulled off the lid and took a sip, then he reached over for a pack of cigarettes. He took his time lighting up.

"You gonna tell us?" Zeus said.

"Why should I?" Nico said.

"So we stop bugging you," Thor said. "So we cross you off our list."

Nico thought about this. Then, "I was at Handsome Jack's all that night. Ask Jack."

"Gambling?" Zeus asked.

"I don't do that anymore. Just drinking. Hanging."

Zeus was looking around. I felt like he wasn't convinced.

"What? You think I took the car to make Herk look bad? Herk Washington makes himself look bad. He doesn't need help from me."

Odin exchanged glances with Zeus.

"Seriously, Herk thinks I did this? Is that who sent you?"

Odin shrugged. "You were upset when he hooked up with Maria."

"If anything, I owe Herk a debt of gratitude for getting me out of that relationship. I have something better now."

"What's that?" Odin said.

Nico put his cigarette in an ashtray and grabbed his phone. He fired it up and then turned it face out, showing an image of him with a blonde girl. I took it and studied the photo. She had wholesome looks, like she could be on a milk commercial.

"This is what I got now. Herk can have Maria, man."

Zeus got a call just then—one of the wig stores, it sounded like. He stepped out onto the porch to speak in private.

Odin eyed me. "What do you think, Isis?"

"She's pretty," I said.

"Thanks," Nico said.

"Not that," Odin said. "The other question."

I frowned.

Odin tipped his head at Nico.

I widened my eyes when I realized what he was getting at. "No way. That is not happening."

"Just academically," Odin said. "How close is he?"

"What are you guys talking about?" Nico asked.

"Nothing you need to worry about," Odin said.

Thor draped an arm over my shoulder. "Nico's not even close. Even I can tell you that, Odin."

"What the hell are you talking about?" Nico asked.

"How do you know?" I asked Thor. Because he was right—Nico was far from my type for watching.

"Instinct, baby," Thor said. "You like a certain gravity."

I studied Thor's face. "How do you know?"

"When I'm, you know, on that end, it's my persona. I think of myself as a stern statue, and I think you like that better. Once when I was watching I smiled, and it cut the energy."

I felt my face grow red, but more, I was kind of flattered. "You put that much thought into it?"

"Of course, baby." Thor nuzzled my ear, breathing hot like I liked. "I put thought into everything with you. All of it."

I smiled in amazement. "Yeah," I said. "I don't like smiley."

"Is there something perverted going on here that I don't know about?" Nico demanded.

"Yes," Odin said. He turned to me. "So we're looking for somebody with stern gravity. But Don Galvano didn't fit the bill. Why? Tell me why, Ice."

"I think this is a bad road to be going down," I said. "I'm off this whole road."

Zeus came back in. "What road?"

"No road," Odin said.

Zeus frowned and headed for the door. I felt a little bad—I didn't like keeping secrets from him, or for Thor and Odin not to know what he was struggling with.

Odin motioned at the coffee and donuts. "Sorry for the inconvenience."

"What the fuck," Nico said. "Call next time. Or maybe just skip me."

We headed down the hallway in silence and took the stairs down.

"With a bit of make-up, Nico could pass for Herk in the dark," I said.

"Agreed," Odin said. "You see anything out there?"

"Nah," Zeus said. "but he certainly...I don't know, he went a little stiff when I asked him, don't you think?"

Odin swung around the rail to the next flight of stairs. "He didn't feel genuine."

We emerged out of Nico's building into the misty February morning, ready to go to Handsome Jack's. Things were getting very *Law & Order* now, but I didn't say that, because my guys hated that show.

Handsome Jack's was a bland sports-themed bar off the beaten trail; its sign proclaimed it a neighborhood pub. "If you have to say you're a neighborhood pub," I observed, "then you're probably not a neighborhood pub."

We asked the hostess for Jack, and she buzzed him with the phone on the hostess stand. A big bald man eyed us from the bar. Zeus nodded at him, and he nodded back. Zeus then picked up a menu to study, but I got the feeling he was really looking the place over.

"That's Len over there," Thor said to me, indicating the bald man. "High-priced muscle."

"Huh," I said.

I felt eyes on me and I looked over to meet Odin's gaze.

"What?"

Odin flicked his glance at Len.

I widened my eyes. "Stop it!"

Odin slung an arm around me and whispered in my ear. "Imagine if we tied him up. And he's stern and powerful, but the way we tie him up, he wouldn't be able to move."

I rolled my eyes.

Odin drew his lips close enough to touch the shell of my ear, evilly using his knowledge of the little places on my body that always got me hot, and continued, "He's tied up, and he can only feast his eyes on your skin as we undress you. All that gravity, caressing your skin with his gaze as we mercilessly use your body for our basest pleasures."

I closed my eyes. I could feel my nipples hardening.

"And you know you shouldn't enjoy it as a stern man watches," he continued, "but it's no use, Isis. Eventually you give over to your pleasure, as you always must."

"Oh, is that so?" I whispered, feeling awkward at how turned on I was, and kind of scared to even look at Len. He wasn't even my type for watching, but closer than Nico.

"You know it's true," Odin said. "You are helpless to us. He, too, would be helpless. And he would watch you give yourself over to us and to the unwelcome intrusion of his gaze," Odin said. "The stern, heavy, uncompromising gaze, penetrating you."

I kept my expression perfectly placid, but my breath sped.

"We would put our hands all over you, and you would shamelessly enjoy it as he watched, helpless as the pleasure builds between your legs—"

I laughed and shoved him away. "You are too much."

"What's going on?" Zeus said.

Odin said, "I think Ice would like us to tie up Len and fuck her in front of him and—"

I gasped.

Zeus had him pressed to the wall before he even finished the sentence.

"—we know now that she likes somebody stern and statue-like," Odin continued.

"We are not playing that. You understand? Do you?"

What was Odin thinking?

"Gentlemen." Handsome Jack came out in a black ball cap and

a mustache to match. "What can I do you for?"

Zeus let Odin down. "I assume Nico told you we were coming."

Handsome Jack smiled suavely. "That he did."

"So you know we're looking into a certain accident. He says you'd vouch for him being here Tuesday night, all night. Though I can't say I love that he called ahead to warn you. Makes a man feel like he's getting something rehearsed."

"You won't have to take my word." Handsome Jack turned and led us through the booth- and fern-filled place to an unfinished back room with pipes zig-zagging across the ceiling. The floor was brown, and the walls were painted a kind of hunter green with portraits of show horses hung here and there. Handsome Jack moved around his desk to a computer and hit a few computer keys. "Tuesday night," he said. "Four feeds. Take a look."

Sure enough, the screen was split into quadrants with Tuesday's date and time stamped at the bottom. He pointed. "There's Nico."

The footage showed Nico drinking at the bar alone at 9:09:57 pm. Jack sped it up and we watched Nico drink and do things on his phone while people walked back and forth behind him. A few stopped to talk with him.

"How long do you keep your records?" Zeus asked.

"I back up a couple months," Jack said.

"Jack's a bookie," Zeus said to me. "Sports."

"That explains the big TVs," I said. And Len, too, but I didn't dare say his name.

"Is Nico still playing?"

"Nah. But he made a lot of friends here when he was. He still likes the sports."

"You do a lot of cash through here?" Odin asked.

"Get in the twenty-first century, man," Jack said. "You think I do cash? I almost never do cash. Strictly PayPal. Pay taxes and everything."

"What?" Odin said.

Jack grinned. "Don't you know? I'm a website designer."

"What the fuck?" Odin said.

Jack grinned and hit a few other keys and up came a website advertising his services. A Google keyword search was a hundred bucks. Site consult was two-hundred.

"Jesus," Zeus said.

"When somebody loses big or consistently, I farm out a simple site to my guy in Romania. They actually get a domain and a site. Keeps things on the up and up."

"This site is sad!" Odin said. "You have flashing shit all over it. Who's gonna fucking believe you're a website designer with a site like this?"

Jack snorted. "You should see their sites."

We got out of there, passing Len on the way out. I could feel the tension rise between my guys, and not about the mystery.

"It's not going to happen," Zeus said out in the parking lot.

"It happens if Ice wants it to happen," Odin said.

"I don't want it to happen," I said.

"You just don't want us to fight," Odin said. "But you would enjoy being fucked in front of a stern, somber man full of gravity. We've established this."

"Is Len your type?" Thor asked.

"No," I said.

"But more than Nico."

Zeus swung into the driver's side and slammed the door. I took the passenger seat this time, just to separate Odin and Zeus. I could see Zeus visibly trying to cool off....and failing. He took a centering breath as he shoved the keys into the ignition. I put my hand on his thigh, feeling shitty for him and the picket fence he'd never get.

He turned to me. "Would you really like that, Isis?"

I wanted to wrap my arms around Zeus, around all my guys. "What I like is all of us happy and in love," I said.

Thor spoke up just then. "Did he seem too compliant? Like he laid his hands on that a little too fast?"

"Yeah," Zeus said. "But Nico did call him. And why would he cover for Nico? Nico has no pull with him. And Jack is good with the Galvanos. Everyone knows that." He started up the car.

"Well," I said, "you have to rule out the dead ends to find the live ones."

A ding sounded, and Odin pulled out his phone. "A text from Herk. Shit."

"What?" I asked.

"Galvano just bought Maria her plane tickets. She leaves the day after tomorrow." Odin looked up. "Two days."

"Damn," Zeus said.

"Don Galvano doesn't want us to solve this," I said, feeling outraged on behalf of Herk. "We should run down the wig places around here."

Odin put away his phone. "Where are we?"

"Twenty-seven-hundred block."

"Hmm."

"What?"

"Tophatter's is on this side of downtown, and they were held up recently. Wigs and cash. Unsolved. I found it when I was researching. It's worth a shot. Head north and right at the light, Zeus."

Zeus pulled out and headed north. The four of us rode in silence, in an unspoken agreement to pretend to focus on the mystery, but we were doing no such thing. The watching thing hung heavy in the air.

I needed to talk to Odin and get him to stop baiting Zeus, even though Zeus had no business making new rules. There was a certain code to how the gang operated, and it didn't include Zeus making up new rules. But Odin needed to stop pushing the watching thing.

I felt scared, like we were on the edge of a whirlpool that had the power to sweep us away.

Chapter Seven

Tophatter's was a massive showroom-style building between a bail bond place and a falafel shop.

We parked and walked in. The place had a musty smell and really ancient signs everywhere that said things like BEST QUALITY ON THE PLANET! in shouty caps. One clerk read the newspaper. *A newspaper!* Even the way the clerks blew off their job was old-fashioned.

It was billed as a costume store with an acre of glamour, according to the sign above the door. They were very sparse acres in terms of customers, though. They seemed to specialize in cowboy outfits, dance and chorus line outfits, and wigs and accessories.

All in all, I got the feeling they'd be out of business soon. Maybe they already were and they were just a front. Life with my guys had taught me how deceiving appearances could be.

A few of the clerks had witnessed the robbery, including a seventy-something woman with unfeasibly tall hair and an aggressively fun attitude. Zeus started asking his questions, and she immediately wanted to know our interest in it, not fooled one second by Zeus's cop-like demeanor.

"We're private investigators with a potentially related case."

That didn't speak to her. Zeus seemed about to get argumentative; quickly I grabbed onto his arm and explained the human angle—the couple in love. Somebody framing our friend with the crashed car. The girl leaving for school doubting him.

Right then and there, she decided she'd help. In fact, she was a lot of help. She recalled five guys—three White, one Black and the other she couldn't tell. She remembered their shoes, their voices. My guys questioned her on where the different guys stood, like their formation.

"The cops certainly didn't ask me about that." She painted the picture and answered questions about who seemed like the leader and what the guns looked like. She called a co-worker to consult and they started going through it all again.

Thor and I wandered around. "Odin needs to stop fucking with Zeus," I said.

"I know. Can you feel it escalating?"

"Yeah." I picked out an orange afro for Thor.

"If Zeus would stop making rules, Odin would stop pushing back," Thor said. "They both need to stop, and they won't, and it's just getting worse." He picked out a wig with long pink hair and bangs for me that was actually quite beautiful.

I put it on, and we looked in the mirror together. "You look like a clown, I'm afraid," I said.

He smiled. "You look fucking amazing."

I grinned. We wore a lot of wigs for robbing banks, but never pink ones. The idea was always to look natural and not stand out.

"Turn around, let them see," Thor said.

I turned to face Zeus and Odin at the counter across the showroom floor. Odin's back was to us, and Zeus was listening intently to the clerks with what I liked to call his charmingly inquisitive expression.

"Too absorbed in the case," I said to Thor.

"No, Zeus sees you. Zeus always sees you." Thor pulled me

flush to his body, my back against his chest, and he arranged the hair over my shoulder. I saw Zeus's thick lips quirk, and then, when the clerks were focused on Odin, he fixed me with a dark, sexy gaze that went right to my belly.

"Stay there where he can see you," Thor said. He went around grabbing clothes. The first was a cowboy jacket with fringes. He put it in front of me and waited.

"What are you doing?"

Finally Zeus looked over. He shook his head no—a minute movement, but Thor and I both saw it.

Next, Thor put a long movie star dress in front of me.

Again Zeus shook his head no.

"What the fuck?"

"He needs me to dress you."

Of course, their weird bandit communication. This was how they robbed banks, too—they spoke to each other without talking.

"He's picking out clothes he needs you to wear for him while he fucks you," Thor said. "You'll have to dress exactly how he wants you."

I bit my lip. It was all a little fucked up, like I was a giant doll for them to play with. Like they would just dress me however they wanted and fuck me however they wanted. Like I was a helpless slave without a will of my own. Like my body was a thing for them to use for their pleasure.

Needless to say, I was wildly turned on. My heart pounded, and I wanted Thor to say it out loud, just like that. Sometimes my guys said things like that to me, and it majorly turned me on.

But instead he was doing bandit communication with Zeus.

Zeus flicked his gaze to the opposite wall.

"Oh," Thor said. He went over and came back to me with a trench coat.

Zeus nodded.

"A trench coat. What am I? Colombo?"

"Oh, goddess," Thor said in his regretful, we-might-have-to-punish-you-now voice. My belly tightened. I waited.

He brought his lips close to my ear. In a deep, testosterone-laden voice he said, "Your body is ours to use. You know that."

My heart began to pound.

"He needs you perfectly prepared so that he can fuck you in that alley out there. Do you understand?"

"Yes," I breathed.

"Fucking you will make him calmer and more centered so that he can solve this mystery." Thor turned me around to face him and drew me in for a kiss, but he didn't kiss me; he stopped with his lips an inch away from mine. I felt the tickle of his nearness, the warmth of his body. He said, "Now go to the changing room in the back of the store, take everything off except your bra and panties, and then you'll put on that coat and come back up here."

"But this is a costume shop. There are sequined things, silk things."

"Oh, goddess," he said. "Zeus needs to fuck you hard and cruel while you're in that trench coat. It's the kind of fuck he needs." He touched a finger to my neck. Just that sent zings to my pelvis.

He slid his finger down to the base of my throat, monitoring the thundering of my heart. I desperately wanted him to talk dirty some more. Like I was a thing to be used. He looked into my eyes, and I knew then that he knew. "He's going to need to take you into the alley and use you like a whore, Isis," he rumbled. "He will need to fuck you and use you carelessly, and for his own pleasure."

"Okay," I whispered.

With a stern gaze he reached around and yanked the tag off the coat. He led me over to the counter where they were talking and slapped the tag onto it. "She's getting the wig, too." He led me back through the maze of racks and dusty displays, past more shouty signs.

He escorted me back to a musty little hallway with a row of changing rooms. "You can keep the boots on. That's all."

I went in and pulled off my pants and blouse and put them in the nylon pop-out shopping bag I kept in my purse. I put the coat over my underwear like he'd instructed. The cool, silky lining felt nice on my skin. I went out and handed the bag to Thor. "Now I'm prepared. Happy?"

"Not really." Thor lowered his voice. "That attitude says you're not prepared."

My blood raced. "What's wrong with my attitude?"

Thor looked around. Nobody inhabited this part of the store. "Get back in there." He pushed me, and I walked back into the dressing room where I'd changed. He went in with me and closed the door. He turned to me and said, in a low and gravelly voice, "Show me."

With trembling fingers I undid the belt and unbuttoned the coat, revealing my underwear. "You're right, it is wrong." He raised his blue eyes to meet mine. "Take it all off. Slowly."

Heart pounding, I let the coat fall to the floor. I reached behind me and unclasped my bra and bared my breasts. Then I removed my panties. I stood there naked and shivering in nothing but boots.

Thor took my underwear, and before I could stop him, he'd produced a switchblade from his satchel and had begun to cut them, altering them. He cut the crotch right out of the panties and then proceeded to saw a large, ragged hole at the center of each bra cup.

"That was my favorite bra!" I protested.

"Now it's my favorite bra. Put it back on."

"There's holes in the most important parts. There's barely any use for underwear like this."

"Oh, there's a use," he said in his rumbly, silky way. "It gives us easy access to what's ours."

My heart stuttered at the dirtiness of it all.

I put the stuff back on.

There's something about wearing underwear that doesn't

cover you properly that feels exciting in a lewd way. I had a bra on, yet my nipples were framed by the fabric, exposed to the cool air. Same with my pussy.

He moved near to me then, touching and squeezing my exposed nipples as he kissed me deeply. I sucked in a breath as he went a little bit hard, roughly rolling them into points as I sucked his tongue, wavering on the knife-edge of pleasure and pain.

"You look so badass like this it blows my mind," he said.

I was thinking I could start getting used to the cut-up underwear when I heard the zing of a tiny chain. I pulled away and saw that he had the alligator nipple clips in his hands.

"Jesus, Thor!" I pushed him away. "Not here!"

He looked at me darkly. "Are you safewording?"

"No," I whispered. "I'm more...."

He gave me a stern look.

"Thor."

"You understand you'll be punished for that."

I closed my eyes. "I just wasn't expecting it," I panted.

"Is that an excuse?" he asked, drawing the belt from the belt loops of the coat.

"Kind of."

"The good thing about a trench coat is the built-in blindfold. So convenient."

"Why do you need a blindfold?" I asked.

"I think you can figure that out." Slowly he tied it around my head. "When you can't see what I'm about to do to you, every nerve ending is more alert. The sensations are more excruciating. Excruciatingly pleasurable."

"What if somebody comes in?"

"You'll have to be quiet," he said. I gasped as I felt the bite of the clamp over my right nipple, then my left. "Good girl." He handed me the coat. "Put it on."

I complied. He buttoned the thing up slowly, tugging the front way more than he needed to. He touched the bottom, but he didn't button down there. Instead he pressed his fingers between my legs, drawing his massive fingers slowly and heavily through my folds, slick with arousal.

I began to move under his touch, needing more. And more. And harder. And up...And up...and every time I moved, the clips sent zings through my body, like little lightning bolts to my brain and pussy both.

"Don't you dare come," he said. "You only get to come with Zeus."

"Okay," I gasped.

"Problem," he said, stroking me.

"Yes," I panted. "I need to come."

"You can't. In fact, I don't think you're even properly prepared for Zeus. I need to think of something else."

"No," I begged. I didn't want him thinking. I didn't want either of us thinking. I reached down and palmed his massive erection, which was easy to find, even with a blindfold.

"Are you trying to distract me? Stalling for time? Hoping Zeus will come and take you right here in this dressing room?"

"Sort of." I unzipped Thor's pants. He hadn't come yet that day, which made him highly distractible.

"Shit," he said as I took out his giant cock. I pictured it in my hand, hard with veins. I ran my thumb over the bulbous head.

"Let go," he grated.

I let go.

He pushed down the belt blindfold so that it was around my neck. I saw right then he was in a state. Thor in this mood was dangerous. A little unpredictable.

He twisted the sash so that it was a little tighter. "On your knees," he grated.

I went down on my knees and looked up, waiting there in my lewd underwear.

His gaze was were all over my body. "You look so fucking beautiful and badass in that, Ice. So wrong and so hot."

I swallowed. I *felt* wrong and hot. Our whole life together was perfectly wrong and hot.

"Spread your knees. Wide."

I complied, spreading my knees, exposing my tender, slick folds to the cool air.

Thor kicked the inside of my knee. "More," he growled.

I went wider, baring myself to his dark, hungry gaze. My clit throbbed with sensation. I felt like I would explode into instant orgasm if he so much as touched me.

"Good." He yanked lightly on the leash, like I was this creature for him to control. A thing under his command, down on my knees for his pleasure.

I practically sparkled with excitement.

"Touch yourself while you suck me, but you will not, *cannot* come."

Eep.

I leaned forward and wrapped my fingers around his root. Slowly and teasingly, I slid my mouth over his cock, sucking, squeezing, while I fingered myself.

"Don't stop touching yourself like that," he gasped. "You need to be primed for Zeus to fuck you."

He rested his hand on the back of my hair, guiding my head, as if the leash weren't enough. I kept on touching myself, trying not to let it feel too good. I concentrated on what I was doing to Thor, going hard at his base with my hand while I did a silky soft thing with my mouth on the rest of his cock, something I'd noticed he enjoyed.

He groaned, cock swelling in my mouth, my throat.

It was too much, asking me not to come in this scenario—especially with this new, mean leash thing.

When I felt the pleasure building, I resorted to reciting months in my head. First how many days were in each month, and then what people's birthdays were in each month. Eventually I had to go to defcon one: presidential birthdays.

"You look so helpless like this. It makes me want to fuck the shit out of you. Hey—" He yanked on my leash. "You with me?" he growled. "Or did you go somewhere?"

I made a sound in the back of my throat.

He hissed out a breath and stroked the back of my hair. "I know this is hard for you, goddess, but I need you to feel everything right now. Feel me fucking your face, baby." With the toe of his boot, he nudged my knees wider. "Push your finger inside yourself, Ice. Make yourself wet for Zeus."

I complied, though I honestly didn't know how I could be wetter.

Thor pushed his cock into my mouth, holding me more firmly now.

"Zeus is upset and emotional. He needs to use you hard, goddess."

He tightened his grip on my hair. His words were having the opposite effect of presidential birthdays. I was so on the edge, I felt half-crazy.

He panted, getting close.

"He's going to throw you against the wall and fuck you like he hates you."

I was pretending to finger myself at this point.

"He'll pull your hair and use your body. And it'll be intense."

I made a sound of protest, because I seriously was going to come if he didn't shut up.

"Shhh, you can do it," he said, stroking my hair. "He'll use your beautiful body for his utter and complete—" He let out a strangled cry and jerked into my mouth one last time, cock pulsing like mad under my grip, shooting cum down my throat, panting, gasping.

He stilled. Moments later, he pulled out and yanked me up by the leash to face him. "Ice." He wiped my lips with his shirt sleeve, then opened up the coat. I whimpered as he pulled the clips off.

"Oh my god," I said, because my nipples were always insanely sensitive after.

He ran his fingers over them, through my dirty cut-out bra. The wild pleasure was building, building. I was about to burst into tears or an orgasm—I didn't know which.

"Your cheeks are this beautiful pink," Thor said. "And your lips are swollen, and your eyes are so wild."

Footsteps in the dressing room hallway.

"Oops," Thor said.

The door opened and there was Zeus. "Where've you been?"

Thor stepped aside.

Zeus swept his gaze up and down me, taking in my pink wig, my cut-up underwear, my aroused, trembly state. "Jesus," he whispered, coming to me. He grabbed my shoulders, looking me over wildly.

I trembled like a sacrifice in front of a rough god. Thor's story had me seriously primed. Thor's stories could do that.

"Please," I pleaded, panting, not knowing what I was saying *please* for.

"Out," he growled at Thor.

Thor left.

He twisted my nipples, watching my eyes.

"Oh, please," I said again.

"Goddess." I wouldn't say he was looked angry, but he didn't seem entirely sane. Zeus undid his pants and took out his cock.

I was panting so hard, I could barely talk. I might have mouthed the word *please*.

"Fuck! Look at you! You are so there." Like a man in a fugue state, he shoved off his shoes and pants and took me into his arms in one mad, brutal motion. "Goddess!" He slammed me against the wall and kissed me sloppily.

I was guessing here that we wouldn't be making it to the alley.

His scratchy shirt was pure madness against my nipples, his scratchy whiskers rough against my cheek.

Without tenderness, he gripped my thigh and lifted my leg, exposing my pussy to his granite-hard bat of a cock.

"I can't...I can't..." *I can't be gentle,* he meant. *I can't be kind.*

"Just...," I whispered, "just...please." *Fuck me,* I meant.

He grabbed his cock and pushed into me, spreading me, filling me, like a jackhammer, thick and hard and unrelenting. He fucked me without mercy, without tenderness, shoving me up roughly against the wall with his hulking mass.

I felt so diffuse, with every molecule in me in perfect contact with the animal part of him, fucking me, using me, needing me. And the rough feeling on my nipples...I knew I couldn't last. Could not last...at which point I broke apart in an explosion of light and madness.

"*Uh-uh-uh,*" Zeus said, fucking me, kissing me all over my face.

He came soon after, emitting a strangled cry. Like a big wounded bull.

I felt such love for him right then, for his big, emotionally raw self. I kissed him, putting all the love I had for him into it.

He buried his face in my neck. "Baby." He held me tight. "Did I hurt you?"

"No way," I said. "You never could."

His chest heaved up and down.

I ran my thumb over his rough whiskers, so worried for our little group. These men were so powerful, but our group was fragile.

I'd be stupid to think otherwise.

"When I saw you standing in here like that," Zeus said, "I don't know—it was like something took me over. Like you were an overinflated balloon I had to burst." He panted softly. "And something inside me...it was so good," he panted. "I so needed..."

I stroked his hair. "It was beyond good," I said. "Um...except for the part where you just compared me to an *overinflated balloon.*"

He smiled his beautiful smile.

I smiled, too. "You think that's a flattering comparison?"

He pulled away and looked at me with this expression of wonder. "Isis—"

"Yes?" I asked.

He was looking at me like he couldn't believe how wondrous I was. Like I was the unicorn version of a woman, so amazing. Or that's what I told myself he was thinking, until he asked, "What is that *underwear* you have on?"

"Oh." The *underwear*. "Thor did that," I said.

"It's so fucked up, it shows how beautiful you are, and it's getting me hard all over again."

I LEANED SIDEWAYS AGAINST THOR IN THE BACK SEAT OF the car, feeling languid and liquid and brain-dead.

"I love you in this wig so much," Thor said. "And this coat."

And mostly the underwear, I was thinking.

Dimly I became aware of clicks coming from the front seat—the sound of guns being checked and loaded. Odin handed Thor back a Glock as Zeus started up the vehicle. "What's going on?" I asked. "What are you doing?"

"We gotta go question some guys who aren't going to want to cooperate. Manny James and his crew. We're not on the best terms."

"The James Gang," I said.

"Don't call them that, goddess," Zeus said. "Our relationship with them is shitty enough."

"The James guys did the wig store stickup," Odin said. "I can't believe even the cops didn't put that together. It's so clearly their style. They always cut the lights first. They always threaten the pets at home."

"They threaten the *pets*?" I said.

Thor nodded. "That's a Kenny James thing. He thinks that's even more effective than threatening the children."

"Who would think that?"

"Kenny James." Thor snorted. "Kenny James is not the brightest bulb on the string. You don't need really strong observation skills to know people will always do more for their kids than their pets given a choice, but Kenny James has these turtles—"

"Failure of empathy," Odin spat. "Kenny James cannot imagine how other people feel."

Thor said, "Odin doesn't think highly of Kenny James."

"Nothing worse than a stupid man with a failure of empathy," Odin said. The level of bitterness in his voice told me he'd had experience with a stupid man with no empathy. He rarely talked about his past, but he'd had some big stuff happen to him. A man doesn't become as hyperperceptive as Odin unless it was how he had to survive.

I said, "You know, the James Gang hating on you guys disproves what Don Galvano said. Like that bit about you guys being stupid as far as the investigation thing? The James gang dislikes you, but they haven't turned you in. You're enemies..."

"We're more frenemies," Zeus said, shoving in a magazine. "Still. One of the wigs stolen in the heist was a B-160 22-inch model, just the one we're looking for. Unlikely they'll cooperate."

"We need that wig ASAP," Odin said. "We need to get it and examine it and see if we can find something. Fibers on it that match the car, that sort of thing. They're not going to like this..."

"Isn't that a little dangerous?

"The James brothers won't snitch to ZOX," Zeus said. "They got a problem, they'll take it up directly with us."

"No, I mean, bursting into the home of heavily armed thugs."

"It'll be fine." Thor smirked and took the safety off his favorite pistol.

Zeus pulled the truck over and had me get into the driver's seat. He got into the passenger side.

Maybe it was the weird tension between Zeus and Odin—I didn't know—but I had a bad feeling. "I don't like this," I said. "Usually we prepare for one of these."

"It's not a bank," Thor said.

"I feel like it's more dangerous. It's not like bank security guards are going to put up much of a fight. But armed guys in their own home..."

"It's not like they sit around watching basketball games with loaded guns next to them."

"How do you know?" I asked. "Not everybody is as balanced and mentally healthy as we are."

"They're sports junkies—I guarantee that's what they're doing," Thor said. "Odin and Zeus will pin them down while I grab the wig and we test it. It's a point and snatch."

"Yeah, things could never go wrong with a point and snatch," I said.

"We got this," Zeus said. "Things going wrong is what we're trained for. You just sit tight."

Sit tight. Wait. Probably for the best, considering my outfit. "What are these guys into these days?"

"Meth sales and some shipping dock rip-offs," Zeus said.

"They've been moving into trailer truck piracy," Odin added. "All-around bad guys."

"The James Gang," I repeated glumly. "All-around bad guys."

Zeus must've heard something in my voice, because he looked over just then. "You good, baby?"

"Fine," I said, but everything felt different.

"I've been itching for a takeover," Odin added.

Zeus had me slow the vehicle on a road full of miniature-looking houses with postage stamp lawns, one of those 1950s developments where they didn't bother trying to make the homes look different, though people had personalized them since then.

"Stop," Zeus said. "The Jameses' house is two up from here—number 2321."

I shoved the thing into park in front of a yellow home with a garden that had a gnome and fawn fairyland theme going. The next home was green. *Viva la shrubberies!* would be their theme. Meanwhile, the James Gang had gone for a *We don't give a fuck* theme with their lawn. And whereas garden gnomeland and *Viva la shrubberies* had nice curtains covering their identical picture windows, the James Gang had crooked curtains over a window that glowed TV blue in the middle of the day.

"Goddess, you'll wait here. You see that dead plant in the front window?"

"Yeah, I see it."

"We'll shoot it out if we want you to drive off, okay? Shooting the dead plant will tell you to drive back to the safehouse, grab some cash, and check into the Radford Inn."

My guys always had to do that—have a safety net for me. It was psychological for them. I nodded my head, as usual. But did they really think I'd just leave them? Luckily it had never come to that.

Odin pulled out his phone. "What date is today?"

"February 13th," Zeus said.

Thor said, "It's Valentine's Day tomorrow."

"Yeah, and we have reservations at La Belle for six-thirty," Zeus said.

"What's La Belle?" Odin asked.

"Seriously? It is the most amazing place. They make a really delicious prix fixe meal—" Zeus turned to me here—"Ice, you are going to love this place. It is really special. It's..." He had this intense look in his eyes, but all he finished with was, "It's just really special."

Meanwhile, Odin announced that the Jameses were probably watching the Knicks. "Let's do it—go, go, go," he said.

Three doors opened and shut, and my guys moved up the sidewalk with such steady speed, they looked almost like they were floating, right up to the moment they split up and melted into the shadows.

I kept my eyes on the picture window, wondering whether their hearts were beating as fast as mine was.

This felt so different from a bank robbery. It wasn't just the danger or the fact that it was on a home. It was something else, and when I really thought about it, I realized the motivation was different—more pure, strange as it seemed. For once my men weren't working for the money or even for the vengeance against ZOX. They were helping Herk.

It made me love them all the more.

It fit them more, too. Helping people was probably why Zeus and Odin got into the field agent game. And Thor, training to be a doctor—that helped people, too. Was that what Zeus hadn't wanted to reveal when he claimed boredom was his reason for wanting to be a P.I.? Was his motivation that he wanted to help people, and he just didn't want to say that?

I just wished they didn't have to run through a house full of all-around bad guys to help Herk.

A dog barked, and it sounded like it was coming from the shrubberies house. The dog obviously heard something—it was really going crazy.

Fuck. That would cut the surprise.

It was then that I heard a gunshot. Shit!

The dog went even crazier. I squeezed the steering wheel with sweaty palms. Probably just a warning. And nobody had shot the plant.

The neighborhood was eerily still.

Bang.

I sat up straight on high alert.

Bang.

The dog barked some more, and that's when the plant exploded. Somebody had shot it.

Fuck!

I put the truck into gear; I was supposed to leave. But how could I? I eased my foot off the brake and rolled, driving toward the house, praying I'd see my guys running out of there with the wig.

The TV continued to flicker and glow. The dog's barks went on.

I stopped just to the side of the house, watching the door hopefully.

They weren't coming. Three shots. Were they hurt? Worse?

Fuck it.

With dreamlike speed, I leaned over to find the Glock Zeus liked to keep taped under the passenger seat. I yanked it out and sat up. That's when I saw the cop car rolling up behind me—no lights and no siren. A cat in the dark.

I stared down at the gun in my hand and quickly shoved it back under the seat. I pulled my jacket more snugly together. Fuck!

The car rolled up slowly. I prayed they wouldn't stop. I smiled sweetly through my panic. *Go*, I thought.

One of the cops eyed me, but they kept going. I watched the cop car roll up to the corner. It stopped, then took a right.

I grabbed the Glock again. My guys would be mad, but I needed to get in there.

What are they going to do, fire you? I said to myself.

Nerves zinging, I snuck up to the porch—it creaked like crazy, but luckily the dog next door hadn't stopped barking his head off.

There was a long vertical window set into the door. I crouched down and looked through at knee level—this was a trick my guys had taught me. My blood ran cold at what I saw: Zeus—with a gun to his head.

He had a gun to the other guy's head, but that didn't make me feel much better. Everybody else was kind of standing around, hands half up, half ready to fight.

The guy holding the weapon on Zeus was Manny James, the James Gang leader. Not good.

I turned and crouched, back against the wall, and tried to think.

I knew that any kind of interruption tended to help break a standoff, but would it be a good break for my guys? Or would it fuck them up to have me burst in? They traditionally freaked out when my safety was at stake.

Still, I had to do something. I inspected the door. You could tell it wasn't quite flush to the frame. Unlocked.

Bottom line: I had to try. I put the gun in my sleeve, took a deep breath, and burst in.

All eyes turned to me. But the guns stayed.

"Ice!" Odin growled. "What are you doing?"

You could cut the tension in the room with a knife. It felt insane—all the fear and testosterone.

Then I got an idea: the one thing that would distract them. I grabbed either side of my trench coat and just ripped it open.

Seven pairs of eyes pivoted to my cut-up underwear.

Nobody said a word.

"I like to call it, underwear by Edward Scissorhands," I said.

Zeus was already moving. He pulled the guy's arm in and twisted, forcing him to drop it. "Fuck!" he said as I closed my coat back up. But he had the gun on Manny. My guys were back in control.

"You didn't follow directions," Thor said.

"Lucky for you!"

"I had it under control," Zeus said.

"Then why did you shoot the plant?"

"Accident," Thor said.

Zeus just glared at me. I didn't know what he hated more—my coming in or my peekaboo show. Or the fact that it worked.

"What the fuck you got that poor girl wearing?" one of the James guys said. "That's the kind of shit you guys go for?"

In a flash, Zeus was moving across the room toward him. "You don't even get to look at her. Not one look."

The guy raised his hands. "Hey, man."

Zeus had his collar. Manny shook away, squaring off, ready to pound Zeus. I was feeling seasick.

It was Odin who stopped the fight. "Come on, Zeus," he said. "We're good here. Let's do this."

I looked at the firearms around the floor. Apparently some people *did* watch sports with loaded weapons. "Did you know there were cops out there?"

"Are you shitting me?" Manny James grumbled. "Did they say anything?"

"No."

Zeus wiped some invisible substance off his sleeve. "Where do you have the wigs? That's all we need here."

"The wigs?" Manny James said. "You're here about the wigs? You come in here like cowboys over the wigs?"

Zeus glared at me, still angry. "So you don't mind us looking at them?"

Manny went to the window and looked out. "The cops left?"

"Yeah," I said. "Came and left."

There was a tense silence.

"You guys got something going on with the cops?" Odin asked.

"It's fine," Manny said. "Just this job a few days back... But the fucking wigs. We'd'a shared the fucking wigs. There's more than we'll ever use. But you're buying us a new fucking plant. What the fuck?"

"We're looking into a thing," Zeus said. "Somebody framing somebody with a wig. If it was you, you wouldn't've let us see them, so..."

"So you can leave now?" Manny barked.

One of the brothers turned the game back up. They were very into the game. They probably had money on it. Maybe they even bet with Handsome Jack. The community was so insular.

"We want to look at the wigs," Zeus said. "Thor needs to run some tests."

One of the other James guys stood up—a young guy with shaggy dark blond hair. He looked more like he should be in a boy band than in a band of hardened criminals. "You're Thor? The doctor?"

Thor nodded.

The guy looked at Manny, who rolled his eyes.

The young one jutted out his chin.

Manny snorted.

Because apparently all bad guys had silent communication methods.

The young guy turned to Thor. "Can you take a look at Brandon? He's got a GSW, and we can't take him in."

"He's a pussy. The bullet's in his muscle," Manny said. "It's a meat tear."

"It looks fucked up to me," the young guy said. "We got a doctor here."

Frankly, I was still stuck on *meat tear.*

"I'd like to look. I'd be happy to." Thor left to get his doctor bag, and I felt the tension in the room go down. I think we were all relieved to find a point of cooperation.

"Where's Kenny?" Zeus asked.

Manny just gave him a hard look.

Odin seemed to perk up. Was it weird Kenny wasn't there?

"Is he around?" Zeus asked.

Manny seemed to get a little taller. Things went slightly more animal kingdom. "You all are getting close to wearing out your welcome." Manny's tone was soft, like hard guys talk when they mean to back up their threats.

Thor returned with his medical bag and followed the young one into the back of the place.

Zeus and Odin and I followed Manny up the stairs into a back bedroom past a row of lockers and locked boxes, probably full of weapons. We stopped at a trunk the size of a large coffin. He unlocked it and pulled up the lid.

The thing was full of wigs.

"Why so many?"

"Convenience," Manny said.

"Right," Zeus said, moving a few aside and pulling up a brunette one. "You mind if we root through?"

"If you don't fuck 'em up."

Zeus went in and started pulling out the brown ones and handing them to me and Odin.

"Buying the disguise the day before a job," I said. "Amateur hour, huh?"

"Exactly," Manny said.

I got the feeling he was just being nice, and that I had probably just made myself sound like an amateur by saying that.

"Sorry about the underwear quip," Manny said.

"It's fine," I said. "I know it's a bit odd."

Zeus shoved two wigs into my hands with a dark glance at Manny. "That's the end of the commentary on Ice's underwear." He loaded us up some more.

Odin scowled. Both he and I had more wigs than we could hold, and we still hadn't found the Herk-hair wig. Manny even started to help. Soon the case was all blonde and red wigs.

"Put 'em back," Zeus said.

"Not there?"

"Nope."

We piled the wigs back in.

Zeus put a protective arm around me, holding me close. "You use any of these yet?" Zeus asked. "Long dark brown hair. Unisex."

"Nah." Manny James described the wigs they had used in the previous week's job. They had trashed them after, but he swore none were the long-hair brown wigs.

Zeus frowned. "You stole a wig like the one we're looking for. It was on the list the Tophatter's had."

"And their word is gospel? Maybe they're looking for some extra insurance money," Manny said.

Zeus didn't buy it. "Would any of your brothers use the wig and not tell you?"

Manny gave him a dark look. "I'd know."

"It was on the list," Zeus said.

"I'd *know*," Manny snapped. The way Manny said that, there was an implied *got it?* spoken through clenched teeth at the end of it.

"Hold on," Odin said. "The Tophatter's heist was right before Christmas. Didn't you all have your New Year's party after that?"

"Yeah, but not up here."

"I hear it was wild as fuck," Odin said.

"New Year's," Manny said, like that was an explanation, and I suppose it was.

"Could someone have come up and helped themselves..."

"To our wigs?" Manny asked. "Is that where you're going? Our guests came up and cracked this lock to get a wig?"

"Was Nico Piazolla here?"

"Nico Piazolla doesn't do locks."

"Was he here?"

"Everybody was here."

"The Gigis?" Odin asked.

"You think the Gigis took the wig?"

"Just getting a sense of the crowd. How about Herk Washington? Bentley?" He rattled off people on and off Herk's list.

Eventually, Manny cut him off. "Yes to all of them. Everybody who's anybody was invited."

Zeus frowned.

After a way-weird silence, Manny added, "...of our people." And I realized we hadn't been invited.

Awk-ward.

We went back to the living room after that and lurked around waiting for Thor. Zeus kept his arm draped around me. The game was still on, and things weren't going the way the James Gang wanted. Finally Thor came out with the young guy, peeling off latex gloves. "He'll live."

We thanked them and got out.

"Front," Zeus growled to me, shoving me toward the vehicle. He really was angry. Even the way he pulled the truck out was angry.

"How can we trust you, Isis?" he said finally. "You fucking go barging in? The plant was shot out. You were to leave if the plant was shot out. That was an agreement we had."

"It was an instruction, not an agreement," I said. "I made a judgment call."

"It's unacceptable. Fuck!" Zeus was gripping the steering wheel so hard, I couldn't believe the thing didn't break right off. "Fuck!"

I could feel my eyes heating with tears. "You guys can rush in after each other, but I can't? Is that it?"

"Yeah," Zeus barked. "That's exactly it."

"You think I would really leave you?"

"We expect it," he said. "And the way you went in there?"

I pulled away from Zeus and wiped my tears, feeling ashamed about flashing the James gang and ashamed about the whole fucking thing. "I couldn't leave you. I made a judgment call."

"You can't do that!" Zeus said. "We are the agents here. We went through years of hard training and got broken a million different ways in the field. Or in the heat of survival and robberies, in the case of Thor. We've seen every way things go wrong and every way to fix it. This is what we do. There are things you are great at, but a judgment call in the heat of action isn't one of them."

Odin spoke up from the back just then. "I thought Ice made a great call."

Zeus glowered into the rearview mirror. "*What*?"

"She broke the standoff," Odin said. "We knew what was

under that coat, but they didn't. They were the ones surprised. It gave you the beat you needed to take Manny's piece."

"I can't believe you're telling her this," Zeus said.

"Plus it was *fucking-g* hilarious," Odin added.

It looked like a vein was about to explode out of Zeus's neck. "You would encourage her to rush in to our defense?"

"I encourage Isis's freedom of decision," Odin said. "She is ours to command in sexual situations, but she's a *fucking-g* standup member of this gang."

I didn't know what to say just then. *Thank you. Stop fighting. Please stop fighting.*

Zeus let out a frustrated growl and turned to me. "Of course you're an equal partner, Ice. But when you go in like that, it changes the dynamic. When it's just us three in danger, we do what we can to save each other. If you're in danger, baby, it's all about you. The three of us don't matter anymore."

"Oh," I said, unable to breathe past the enormity of what he was telling me.

"I agree it's important you know that," Odin said. "The more informed you are, the better, but we shouldn't make rules for you that we wouldn't follow. Rules are never smarter than people."

"This is just you being fucked up about rules," Zeus said.

"No," Odin growled, "this is you, Zeus, trying to fucking control us."

"Enough," Thor said.

"Isis is a full partner," Odin continued, "not a possession to be hoarded or a robot to be controlled."

"Oh my god, you guys!" I said. "Stop it!

Zeus sucked in a deep, angry-sounding breath.

My heart pounded. It had begun to rain, naturally, so on top of everything else, we could barely see out the windows. We should probably be hungry; we hadn't had dinner, but I was too upset to eat. I'm sure we all were.

We headed toward home in silence, except for the sound of wipers squeeching back and forth.

"Edward Scissorhands?" Thor finally said.

Odin snorted. "What must they think? I mean, *what* must they *think*? Her in that underwear."

"Oh my god," I said.

"It was *fucking-g* hilarious," Odin said.

"Yeah, it was pretty funny," Thor said. "So fucked up. That was the best part."

I swallowed back a smile and looked at Zeus.

Not amused.

I was grateful when Thor asked about the wig and they got on to talking about the mystery again. Something we could all agree on.

Zeus said, "They throw the wigs away after they're done using them—did you catch that, Odin?"

A little bit of an olive branch, engaging Odin like that.

"And our wig wasn't there," Odin said.

"Which tells me one of them used our wig," Zeus continued, "because I don't see those clerks lying about it being one of the stolen ones. If the wig was taken, the wig was taken. The James Gang had the wig at one point, and now they don't."

"There was the *fucking-g* party, though," Odin said. "I bet everyone on Herk's list was there."

"Could somebody have snuck up to the bedroom?" I ask.

"Have you ever had anybody describe one of their New Year's parties to you?" Odin said. "It's a hundred or so people in a blind drunk tear. They don't know what the fuck happens at their parties, and if somebody wanted to go up there, they wouldn't have to sneak. They could saw a hole in the ceiling and climb through that way and the James brothers wouldn't notice. And getting through that lock, Angel could crack it with her hands tied behind her back."

"Why would Angel do that?"

"She'd do it if somebody challenged her. She's proud like that. Anyways, at a party like that, she's not the only one who can twist open a lock. She's the fastest, but not the only."

"We should eat at Guvvey's," Thor said. "Thursday night. Sushi night. You know the Gigis are there. They were at the party. They know Herk's people."

So scratch the part about us being too upset to eat.

"Um, stopping by the house first to change?"

"It would serve you right to make you wear that from now on," Zeus said. And with that the tension dissipated a little bit more.

"They probably wouldn't let me in like this. Guvvey's has standards," I reminded him.

He put on the blinker when we hit the turnoff that went to our house.

Odin asked Thor about the James Gang gunshot wound patient. Thor said that the wound hadn't been cleaned properly and it was infected. He'd administered shots for it and cleaned it. The boy-band-looking kid who'd spoken up and brought Thor back there was apparently Noel James.

"You left it good with Noel?" Zeus asked Thor.

"Very good."

"One fucking reasonable James," Odin said. "The rest of them are crazy. Did he say anything about Kenny James?"

"What about him?"

"They were just prickly about him, and he wasn't there," Odin said. "You feel how prickly they were?"

"I felt it," I said. "Something's definitely up with Kenny James."

Chapter Nine

WHEN YOU READ STUFFY OLD NOVELS OF A CERTAIN kind, especially those set in old-timey London, the characters will often have a "club" that they frequent. These are typically special and private and beautifully decorated, as opposed to a public house or pub where all the riffraff can go.

That's what Guvvey's was for the criminal element of Los Angeles. Though instead of overstuffed chairs and museum-esque portraits of men, there were mod blue globe lights and red seating and walls covered with weirdly colorized wildlife photo murals, and not the kind with cute woodland animals, either. No, the human predators of Los Angeles enjoyed frequenting a place lined with photo murals of lions and tigers killing beautiful antelopes and other living things.

The place was in a downtown building on an upper floor that didn't technically exist or have a number. You got there via tunnels and elevators. The dress code called for nice clothes—suits, ties, dresses, that sort of thing, and the criminals went all-out. I got the feeling it was one of the few places they felt like they could flaunt their ill-gotten gains. Now and then people came in without dressing up; as Zeus pointed out, it was basically a club for people who don't like following rules, so what were they going to do?

For this night I'd chosen a blue cocktail-length gown in a wrap-around style. It had fun cutaways on the sleeves. My guys were in sport coats. Odin had gone with plaid in one of his endless and futile attempts to not look hot. We walked in as a gang, the four of us looking tight and together for all the world to see.

In truth, I'd never felt so deeply threatened. Threats from the outside we could handle. But this rift between Odin and Zeus felt deep and dangerous. Both Zeus and Odin were getting way too emotional.

Sure enough the Gigis were there, or at least their leader, Macy, was there, up at the bar, which meant the rest of her jewel thief comrades were nearby. She was looking awesome in a purple pantsuit with high white boots, and she'd let her hair go afro, and she was chatting up some young stud with bleached dreadlocks.

The Gigis had tried to recruit me once, which pissed my guys off, but we were all on more friendly terms lately.

We slid into our favorite booth and put in our drink and food orders, to which Odin added a drink for Macy Gigi.

Our food order consisted of "yes," because when you ordered food at Guvvey's, you got whatever they were making, which, as established, was sushi that night.

While Thor and Odin questioned the waiter on who'd been in recently, Zeus put his arm around me. "I hope you don't think I regard you as a possession, goddess," he said softly. "Or like you can't think for yourself."

"I know." I rested my hand on his cheek.

"I would never think it," he said. "I didn't mean to come down on you. It's just that I don't know what I'd do if…"

"It's okay, Zeus. It was about you protecting me. I know that."

When Macy got her drink, she smiled over at us, and a few minutes later she was strolling up to our booth with Angel Gigi at her side.

"The sheep farmer and her swains, out on the town," Macy said.

I rolled my eyes as we made room at the booth. The sheep farmer bit I could've lived without, though I did like *her swains.*

Angel was rocking her usual wild style, which tonight was a vintage black party dress and a tiara, and I had no doubt the thing was studded with real diamonds—all stolen, probably pirate-treasure-trove quality, because that was how the Gigis rolled.

"Is it true you're looking into Herk's joyride?" Angel asked.

Zeus groaned. "Who's saying that?"

"Everyone," Angel said.

"What are they saying?" Odin asked her.

Gigi Macy sipped her champagne. "Well, for one thing, of the people who know Herk, nobody thinks he did it. Being that it's a Corvette and all."

"So fucking sad," Angel said. "Poor Herk had to always act like he liked the thing. And now he can't be like, *I'd never be caught dead in your dumbass car.*"

"Who do you think did it?" Odin asked. "If you had to put your money on somebody right now."

"You crowdsourcing this thing?" Macy asked. "That's your big investigative style?"

Odin raised his brows, unamused. He had a real love-hate relationship with the Gigis.

Macy laughed. "My money would be on Decker Dormand. He's been battling Herk for the corners in the Oakford Lanes area. If Herk links up with the mob suddenly, Herk'll be a fuck of a lot stronger going into that fight."

Zeus straightened up. "You think if Herk marries Maria he'll merge his business interests with Galvano's in some way?"

She shrugged. "There's rumors."

"Of what, exactly?"

"Consolidation," she said. "Just natural to think it'll happen. For example, Galvano has muscle, Herk has muscle. Two separate silos of muscle. And suddenly they're at Christmas dinner together and maybe they're talking about their operations, like, why do I have a dozen guys on my payroll to go out and bust heads when you have a dozen guys on your payroll?"

"Well, that *is* a traditional thing for families to discuss around the Yule log," I said.

Thor smiled and kicked me.

I smiled back. In spite of their calm, collected demeanor, my guys were concentrating fervently on the investigation.

"The other theory out there is that Galvano planned to hand over a little piece of his mafia action to whoever married Maria," Macy said. "I heard that one."

"Not to a Puerto Rican brother," Angel said. "No way. Who said that?"

Macy shrugged. "The grapevine said it."

"I'll believe it when I see it," Angel said.

I noticed that Zeus had taken out the list of names Herk had made. He slid it across the table to Macy. "Anything pop out here for you?"

"These are your suspects?" she asked.

"A subset of them."

"Subset, huh." She set a silver-painted fingernail on Nico Piazolla. "Not Nico. He's all over Sophia Viga. He's whipped on her."

"You believe it?" Odin asked.

They both said yes, convincingly.

"Sophia Viga's a married woman. Doesn't her husband have a problem with all this?" Thor asked.

"They say she's moving out. I don't know, though," Angel said. "Sophia's so heavy into her Guccis and Pradas, I don't see her leaving her husband for Nico Piazolla. I mean, Nico does well for himself, but he's a bad bet, what with the gambling."

"He's clean of that," Macy said. "Everyone knows. Even Handsome Jack says."

Angel sniffed. "Handsome Jack should be the last person to call somebody clean of gambling. Handsome Jack has built his life on people's inability to quit."

Macy hit another name with her silver claw—the James brothers. "Kenny James would do it. Kenny fucking hates Herk."

Odin and Zeus exchanged glances.

"Did you talk to him yet?" Macy asked.

"We were over there, but Kenny wasn't there," Thor said. "Were you all at their party for New Year's?"

The two Gigis exchanged mischievous glances. I smiled, wishing I knew what they were thinking, and remembering what those bonds were like. Wishing I had girlfriends. Missing my sisters. I never missed my sisters so much as when the Gigis were around, because that's how my sisters and I had been. Tight like that.

"Fuck," Angel said finally, positively sparkling at Macy.

"You see anyone go up onto the second floor?" Zeus asked. "Or were you up there?"

Angel twirled her straw in her drink. "One level of that party was fucked up enough for me."

It was right then that Nico Piazolla himself appeared at the table, as if out of nowhere. He glanced down at the list before Zeus got a chance to take it away. "Making any headway?" Nico asked.

"Oh yeah," Zeus said mysteriously.

Angel turned to Nico. "You were engaged to Maria. Were you promised any kind of wedding gift? Like a piece of the Galvano action?"

"What is this? 1920s Sicily?" Nico snorted and sat. "No. Not that I know of." There was this silence where he looked around the table, curious. "So really, who do you have? Who are you looking at?"

"You think you can help?" Odin's fake casual tone didn't fool me.

Nico nodded at the sheet. "Did I see the word James on there?"

There was a strained silence. My guys apparently didn't like that he'd peeked.

"What if you did see it?" Odin said.

"Well, I'm just saying, it would add up," Nico said. "Herk and the James brothers are on the outs. Especially Kenny James. Kenny and Herk..."

"Too true," said Angel.

"What about Kenny and Herk?" Zeus asked.

"Some shit between Herk's sister and Kenny," Macy said. "Kenny blames him for wrecking their relationship. Wasn't Herk's fault, but that's Kenny. Man's had a fixation on Herk ever since."

"Serious fixation," Nico said.

"Huh," Zeus said, like this was all news to him. Right then I knew it wasn't, and that Zeus was working a few steps ahead.

The bunch of us gossiped about Kenny James for a while, then the talk turned to people I didn't know. They left when our food came.

"Interesting," Zeus said simply.

Odin passed the spicy ginger. "Very interesting. Nico's...a little chatty. And where the fuck is Kenny? I think we need to talk to Kenny."

Zeus scanned the room like a rangy bear. "Right."

We traded sushi around until we all had only our favorites. There was so much, I could barely finish mine. I ordered another drink and turned sideways, leaning back on Odin. He snaked a hand around my waist and kissed me.

Zeus got up. "I'm going to call Herk and ask him about Kenny."

He walked off.

Odin and Thor watched him move through the crowd; he paused to slap hands with a guy and kept on, disappearing around the bar.

"This proprietary shit cannot stand," Odin said. "Acting like your fucking husband."

I sat up. "What do you mean?"

"That's why he got up and stormed off just now," Odin said. "Because I'm putting my hands on you while he's stuck on the other side of Thor, and he thinks I'm going to finger you, which I am, and he's pissed as hell."

Chapter Ten

"Oh, is that your plan?" I teased Odin. "That's your big plan?"

"Shhhh," he said, pulling the side of the skirt part of my dress aside under the table.

Thor patted his thigh. "Put your right leg up here, baby."

I looked over where Zeus disappeared to.

"He's a big boy," Odin said. "He'll get over it. And I have an agenda."

"What?"

Thor grabbed my leg and nestled it on his lap.

Energy shot clear through to my core as Odin slid soft fingers over my cotton-clad pussy. "Oh my god," I whispered.

Odin trailed two fingers up my bare thigh. "So far, we have stern, statue like, and full of gravity. And tied up. What else?"

"I am not completing this profile. You have to stop this madness with Zeus."

"Zeus needs to stop the madness," Odin said. "Zeus can't stop us from doing something we three want to do."

"It's upsetting him." I sucked in a breath as he slid his fingers under my panties, edging toward my sex.

"You shouldn't have changed your underwear."

"Why do you keep pushing him?" I asked. "It threatens the group."

"You think what I'm doing threatens the group?" Odin growled. "Zeus is the one threatening the group. Open your eyes, Ice. First he doesn't want a watcher. Now he doesn't want my hands on you without him involved? Think about that," he said. "Is that what we do? You want us to change how we are?"

"Fuck, no," I said. "I like us wild and free, but I want to help Zeus."

Odin trailed his clever fingers up and down my thigh. "It doesn't help Zeus if we let him change us," Odin said. "He needs us to stand tall on this."

"It's true," Thor said, as he took off my shoe and started massaging my toes.

"He's going through something, I get it." Odin stroked his thick finger over my swollen, needy nub. "You know what we are, baby?"

"Sex-crazed?"

"Outlaws." Odin pushed two huge fingers into me then, filling me gloriously. I whimpered, there in the dark booth in the dark corner of an outlaw bar that wasn't supposed to exist. Slowly he pulled them out, then pushed them back in. "We're brave and fierce, and we respect no law. Zeus needs to find his way back to that," he whispered.

"Yes." I rocked along with his motion, in and out, in and out.

"Outlaws don't have to follow rules. I'd lay down my life for him, but nobody puts me in a cage with their *fucking-g* rules." He continued to fuck me and stroke me.

Odin made a certain amount of sense. And I didn't want to be in a cage of rules, either. But there was something else...something...I grabbed his wrist. "We have to get back to helping Herk. Whoever did it could be destroying the evidence right now."

"We want it that way," Odin said. "You think Zeus let Nico see the list by accident? Nico has the biggest fucking mouth. Whoever did it is going to tell us so."

His warm palm moved back up the inside of my thigh. "Drink your drink. Act normal," he said.

I took a drink as he pushed his other hand under my dress and took hold of my nipple. "Oh my god," I said.

"You so love an audience," he whispered, finding my needy core full-on now, invading my wet sex with magical fingers.

My belly tightened. My eyes drifted shut.

"Stern, statue like. We need more."

Thor glided a fingernail up and down the sole of my foot. The wild, delicious contrast of sharp, bright scratches on my foot with the dark, languorous strokes between my legs put my every nerve ending onto high alert.

"You guys," I breathed, mind melting.

But of course they continued, stoking up my excitement like crazy.

"Look at her face—she's about to come," Thor said. "Don't you dare come, Ice."

"No coming is a rule," I gasped.

"It's different, and you know it, goddess," Odin said. "And if you come before I tell you that you can, you will be punished." He lowered his voice. "It will be the kind of punishment where you have to sleep for hours afterward."

Gulp.

He wasn't kidding around about the sleep. Spending a couple of hours wrung out on the knife edge of pain and pleasure could be more tiring than running a marathon, except let's just say you got something way better at the finish line than a Dixie cup of Gatorade.

Awesome as the prospect was, I resolved not to come. I wanted to be in on the investigation! With a shaking hand I took hold of my drink and took a sip, trying to focus on this simple motor skill operation as a way to block Odin's clever machinations.

"I can feel you so swollen with pleasure now," Odin said. "You're ready to go, aren't you?"

"Yes," I breathed. He slowed, and I whimpered—a little bit protest, a little bit gratitude.

"Two more words," he said. "And you can have your orgasm without punishment."

I stared out at the crowd, thankful for our dark cover.

Thor sneered. "No, no, no. Look at me while he touches you." He slid a fingernail harder down my foot. I squirmed.

Odin tightened his arms around me. "Your body is ours. We own you and your pleasure," he whispered.

Thor watched me with a steady blue gaze. "And no thinking about the months, either. Now let's have the rest. Stern. Statue like. What else? Who here would fit the bill?"

I swam in feeling as he drew a wicked nail down my tender sole. "Probably nobody here," I said.

"Why?" Thor asked. "You haven't even seen everyone here."

"Aha," Odin said. "A noncriminal."

"No, not exactly," I protested.

Odin made his stroke hard and flat. I writhed with sensation. "I can feel you feeling my fingers. Each with hundreds of finger-print ridges, invading your silky pussy. You are going to come, goddess, and the punishment will last for hours. And you will not get to play Sherlock with us."

Thor scratched a sharp line across the sole of my foot. "Ow!" My eyes flew open and I stared at him. His smile managed to look both evil and innocent. He knew exactly how much pain got me off.

"He'll do it again."

"He can't," I breathed.

Odin whispered in my ear. "You are going to come, very soon." He pushed in his fingers again, curling them slightly inside of me. I was panting, gasping. "You are powerless against this level of pleasure. I am going to make you come. And if you do not reveal more about your type for watching, I will take you right home."

"He'll just whip it out of you at home." Thor said sadly. "You don't get to keep secrets from us."

I gasped as Odin moved his fingers and pushed on a *certain* spot...*the* certain spot. "Okay, okay, okay!"

Thor held my gaze. "You are so ready." He slid his hands all over my foot, moving up to my calf. "Give it up, baby."

Odin pressed on my clit with his thumb, rubbing and fucking me. "It is useless to fight this. You are already beginning to milk my fingers. You are already there, goddess. There is still time..."

He was right—my orgasm built like a tidal wave deep inside me. I was going to come, and then it would be too late. "Authoritarian," I gasped. "Disapproving!" I burst into a zillion shards of pleasure, coming shamelessly in the crowded nightclub.

"Mmmm." Odin nuzzled my hair, slowing his cruel and masterful touch. "Was that so hard?"

He sounded far away. The world was far away. Reality, normality, all of it. Far, far away.

Thor said, "You are so beautiful when you come. Like weeping turned inside out."

Odin grabbed a paper napkin and wiped between my legs. "Authoritarian and disapproving."

"I can't believe I told you," I said.

"I can," Odin said, and his beautiful lips spread in a slow smile.

I reached up and touched his moppy, curly hair. "I agree we don't want to change, but you guys need to go a little easier on Zeus, okay?" I looked over at Thor. "Okay?"

They scoffed at that and razzed me a bit more about my type; they had quite the profile going at this point, but they shut it down when Zeus returned. My guys spent the rest of the night circulating and chatting people up, sometimes with me along.

Three hours later we were stumbling out of the elevator and

heading into the tunnel that led to the parking garage where our car was.

Or at least I was stumbling out of there, having consumed three glasses of champagne, which was one over my limit. The guys had mostly consumed gossip. In the stairwell up, I bemoaned the fact that we hadn't gotten any valuable leads.

"Are you kidding? It was a valuable night," Zeus said.

Thor held the door open for me, and we headed into the cavernous fifth floor of the ramp. It was four in the morning. There were only a few cars scattered around. I spotted our car glinting across the way. I wanted nothing more than to collapse inside it.

I grabbed onto Zeus's arm and smiled up at him. "If I fall asleep on the way home, will you carry me into my bed?"

He didn't answer or even smile; something was wrong.

"What?"

"Smell," he grated.

Odin stiffened.

"What?"

Zeus pulled me around and slammed me up against a concrete pillar; he clapped his hands over my ears and covered me with his body.

I was opening my mouth to protest when an explosion ripped through the place.

I clutched onto his sports jacket as smoke filled the place. Car alarms blared. There was a big crash—part of the ceiling?

"Was that our car?" I asked.

Zeus was running his hands all over my body. "You okay, baby? Anything hurt?"

"I'm fine, but was that our car?" I asked again.

Odin and Thor were behind another concrete pillar, guns drawn. They moved to join us. "Take her back to the club," Zeus said to Thor.

"Come on," Thor said.

"B-but—"

Thor pulled me back into the stairwell with uncharacteristic force. We raced down. I could barely walk, my legs were shaking so much. "Was that our car? Was our car supposed to blow up with us in it?"

"Don't think about it," Thor said.

"How can I *not* think about it?"

He squeezed my hand, pulling me down the steps. "You're okay," he said. "And we're okay."

"Why'd they stay up there?"

"They think that whoever did the car is still around," he said.

Thor brought me all the way back to the club. We found the Gigis at a table near the giant window. "Thought you left," Jenny said.

"Trouble," Thor said. "Someone did our car."

Macy's lips parted. "As in blew it up?"

Thor gave her a dark look.

"But nobody was in it, right?" Jenny said.

I shook my head. "Zeus smelled it."

"You guys sticking around?" Thor said. "We don't want Ice alone."

"I'm fine," I said.

Angel looped an arm around my shoulder. "We're sticking around. Maybe I'll even let her wear my tiara."

Thor took off.

I put my hand to my chest. "I feel like my heart's going to pound right out of my chest."

"How close were you?" Macy asked.

"Across the garage. If Zeus hadn't smelled it..."

"But he did."

"Fuck," Jenny said. "Somebody doesn't like your investigation."

Macy sniffed and crossed her legs, white boots shining. "If I framed one of L.A.'s toughest motherfuckers for crashing the

Corvette of another of L.A.'s most dangerous motherfuckers, I'd be blowing up cars, too."

"You think this is somebody freaking out?"

"Of course," she said. "To go after you that? With you *there*? Shit."

Jenny pointed at me with a toothpick. "Which means your boy toys have another clue—the culprit is batshit crazy."

"Which rules out, oh, maybe fifty percent of the people here," Angel said.

A glass of champagne arrived. "Drink up, girlfriend," Jenny said.

I took it and swirled the liquid. "We almost died just now."

"But you didn't," Angel said.

"I hate this," I said. "They think the person who did it was still out there."

"Blowing up a car is a coward's move," Macy said. "I promise you, the doer ran away when they saw that it didn't work."

"One more minute, and we would've been in there," I said.

"You're okay. Shit happens."

"Shit happens?"

Macy grinned. "Drink."

I took a sip and then pushed it away. "All I want right now is to be on the couch with a bowl of popcorn and one of the stupid superhero movies those guys always want to watch. I just want to hide together. I love those guys so much."

"They'll be okay," Jenny said. "Drink."

"I probably shouldn't have any more. I already had three."

"And how drunk are you?"

"Not at all. I feel sober."

Angel took off her tiara. "Car bomb'll do that to you. Drink up and I'll let you wear it."

"It's okay."

"I saw you looking at it. You know you want to wear it. Go on —bottoms up."

I took another sip.

"Good enough." She handed it to me, and I put it on.

"Perfect." She smiled. "Is that better?"

"A little."

"A tiara always makes you feel better. It makes *me* feel better every day."

I looked at her anew just then. I'd always thought the Gigis had everything together, but I guess everyone has their demons, even pretty, talented safecrackers with the best jewels in the world. "Thanks."

Macy said, "I would *not* want to be that person right now. Can you imagine how they're freaking?"

"You know as well as I do that anybody who wants to hurt my guys has a trump card to play." I meant dropping a dime to the Feds and getting ZOX on their ass.

Angel pursed her pretty lips. "Huge fucking death wish, anyone who does that."

"What are we doing?" I asked. "Maybe we need to rethink things."

"You have three hot husbands, Isis," Macy said. "What exactly do you want to rethink here?"

Jenny smiled. "Three husbands, bitch. You're like a hero to us."

"I'd like to avoid the car bombs."

"Shit." Jenny fixed her gaze over my shoulder. I turned to see a dark-haired man in a fine tuxedo strolling toward us. Even in the chaos of Guvvey's, everybody seemed aware of him—their faces and bodies turning toward him like sunflowers, orienting to the light. The ripple of attention following him was like a living thing. "Who is that?"

"Stamos Strong," Jenny said. "He owns this place."

"I've never seen him here," I said.

"Very reclusive," Angel said. "Very hot, very rich, very reclusive."

"Whoa," Jenny said as he neared, straightening her dress.

He came up to side. "You're Isis?" Mr. Strong said.

I nodded.

He held out a hand and introduced himself to me, and then to the Gigis. "I just heard what happened," he said. "I want to personally apologize, and let you know I put a team on all the feeds from the garage. We haven't turned up any decent images of your culprit, but you go ahead and tell your men that Guvvey's will assist in any way possible."

"Thank you," I said.

He bid us goodnight and left the way he came, in a wake of adoring gazes.

"He's even hotter up close," Jenny sighed.

"Mother of fuck." Angel slammed her drink. "The one time Stamos Strong comes around, and you were wearing my tiara."

I smiled.

Jenny pushed the champagne toward me. "Drink. Breathe."

"I feel too fucked up."

"Notice a color," Macy said.

"Excuse me?"

"When we're on a hard job, or like when things are going wrong on a job, I look around and pick out a color to notice," she said. "And I really take it in. I pick out one color. Go on, do it."

I focused on the lime green leaves of one of the trees on the wall mural.

"Really notice it," she said. "Let it into yourself."

It actually seemed to work—my heartbeat felt slower. I felt more substantial, somehow. I regarded Macy with surprise. She grinned. "You have to stay calm in our line of work. And here's what else—your guys are the best. You need to trust them."

I nodded, feeling better until Jenny said, "We heard about your peepshow at the James brothers' place."

"Oh my god," I said.

They teased me about it, assuring me that yes, everybody in

Guvvey's probably knew about it. It took my mind off the close call for about ten seconds, so that was something.

I asked Macy about Matteo, her former boyfriend. She'd kicked his ass to the curb after he'd cheated on her, but last I heard, they were back on speaking terms. She told me a long, funny story where things were going better...until he started mansplaining during a crime spree they'd let him tag along for.

"Back in the doghouse," Macy said.

An hour later Zeus was there, beelining across the place. He pulled me up off my chair into a giant bear hug. "Baby," he said. "Fuck, I'm so sorry."

"It's okay, baby," I whispered into his ear. "We're okay."

It didn't ease him. He was caught in his vast, deep animal emotions, and I wanted to tell him he was beautiful, but the word seemed so inadequate.

The Gigis gave Zeus and me a ride home, and we told him about the Stamos Strong visit. To hear them talk about it, you'd think the pope himself had stopped by.

Odin and Thor were apparently off looking into something. When we got back home, Zeus told me they'd returned to the James Gang's place, looking to see whether Kenny James was there.

"It's three in the morning," I said.

"They're up," he said, pulling me onto his lap on the couch. "But I wanted to get you out of there."

Odin and Thor came back a bit later. They said Kenny James wasn't around, but they were very suspicious of him at this point.

"Kenny James loves to blow up cars," Odin said.

Thor grabbed a bag of cheese curls, his favorite middle-of-the-night snack. "I knew the James brothers were hiding something. Even I could see it. It's something with Kenny."

Chapter Eleven

WE HEADED BACK TO THE OFFICE THE NEXT DAY FOR another meeting with Herk.

I'll admit, heading out to the office was not on my list of top ten most-appealing things to do after somebody tries to blow up your car with you in it, but my guys were keen on moving forward with the investigation, and Zeus had this thing about showing up at the office every day.

So we showed up.

I sat on the desk as they went around turning on the lights and clearing the place. And there was no Coco Chanel suit, either. Instead I wore my favorite sweater and jeans. Comfort clothes. I was shaken.

I'd always thought they couldn't be in more trouble than they were already in, sort of the way you can't get more pregnant than pregnant. They were internationally wanted fugitives, after all; could you get more wanted than that?

Yes, apparently you could. Apparently other criminals could turn on you, too. It was a vast and exciting new panorama of enemies to make. The devious kind that knew where you hung out. The kind that would want to blow up your car, and probably had the perfect bomb-making materials in the closet where most people kept their wrapping paper and Christmas tree ornaments.

Thor came over and took my hand and kissed it. "We're okay," he said.

I managed a weak smile. We were so far from okay it wasn't even funny. We weren't okay on the inside, what with the rift between Zeus and Odin, and we weren't okay on the outside.

But we were all determined to help Herk. Like we couldn't have a normal life, but our pal Herk could.

Herk brought Maria Galvano along to the meeting. She had long black hair and decal nails, and she was a biology major at USC, or had been before the transfer to Oxford. I'd met her once or twice at Guvvey's, and I'd always liked her. She seemed skeptical, though.

"You seriously think it's Kenny fucking James?" she said once Zeus had caught them up on the night's events. "That Kenny James would take my dad's car..."

"It wasn't *me!*" Herk said.

"I believe you, but..." Maria paused. "Kenny James? With a wig? The candlestick, the library..."

Herk sighed impatiently. Maria wanted to believe him, but she didn't.

"We'll figure it out," I said.

"Sorry, I don't mean to sound impatient. I just don't have much time. I have to pack. I have to get clothes for a whole different climate."

"Your dad won't make you go once he sees he's being played," Herk said.

Odin asked him about his history with Kenny James, and Herk went into a long saga about his younger sister dating Kenny James. When she'd discovered Kenny was having an affair, she'd dumped him. After that, Kenny showed up at her house—repeatedly— pleading his case. He'd gotten a little scary at one point, and she'd called Herk, who'd come by and beat the crap out of Kenny.

"In front of her," Maria said.

"Damn right I beat his ass in front of her," Herk said. "So she could see him cry like a little wimp and not want him back. A girl doesn't want a guy once she sees him weep from a beating. It's evolutionary, man."

"Evolutionary in a man's mind," Maria said. I smiled in solidarity, even though I kind of didn't agree with her.

"Fuck yeah," Herk said. "And now I'm gonna tear his fucking face off. I mean that literally, man." He stabbed a finger at Zeus. "You find him, and I will take care of the rest. And he's going to apologize to the Don, and then he's going to apologize to Maria and kiss the ground she walks on."

A seemingly tall order for a man with no face, but that wasn't the kind of detail you pointed out at a time like this.

He turned to her, then. "Fucking put you through this. Put us through this. It's not right."

"I know, baby," she said.

Herk pulled her tight and kissed her. "I can't believe Kenny would do that."

"Either way, we really appreciate your trying to figure this out," Maria said. "If there is any way we can help..."

Zeus asked her what she was doing, and she told him she was shipping some boxes, then heading off to the mall.

"Don't start shipping things yet," Herk said.

"I have to be practical," Maria said.

"We're going to figure this out."

"I can't just drop out of college in the meantime," she said.

"Your dad still sends you around with muscle, right?" Zeus asked.

"Sure," she said. "I got two guys."

Zeus crossed his arms. "Can Ice come?"

"But the investigation! I need to help," I protested.

"Not when the explosions start," Odin said. "This guy's getting desperate."

"And you know what today is?" Zeus said. "You'll require a new dress."

"A new dress?" I said. "You think that'll make it okay to not include me? Because, wow, I get a new dress?" I could barely swallow my anger.

"When things start blowing up?" Zeus said. "Damn right we're not including you."

"I'm an important part of this team," I said, looking my bandits in the eye—Zeus, Odin, Thor. No go. All I saw was a united front of caveman thinking. Even Thor wasn't going for it. The car bomb had really spooked them. "This is our thing. Ours together."

"We're hunting, baby," Zeus said. "You're amazing at the questioning, but we're hunting a hunter. Somebody who knows we're after him. Somebody who is looking at a very undesirable fate if he is to be caught."

I knew this was an argument I wouldn't win.

"Come along with me," Maria said. "It'll be fun."

I turned to her. "I know. It's just—"

Her wistful look told me she got it. "I know."

"Man's got nothing to lose," Odin said.

"Fine," I said.

"Bring something to do while I deal with shipping and customs forms, and we'll have some fun after that," Maria said.

<h1 style="text-align:center">Chapter Twelve</h1>

Having two bodyguards trailing you was a lot different from being in the God Pack. My guys were all about flanking me and hanging arms around me and being the romantic unit. Treating me like a princess.

But when you were an actual crime figure's daughter, like Maria, the bodyguards were discreet. And the biggest difference: they took orders instead of giving them. Once we got into the freight place, she had them carrying boxes, filling out forms, running for coffee.

"I hope that didn't seem insulting before, like I didn't want to come," I said.

"I get it," Maria said. "My dad is Carmine Galvano. Do you know how much I'm shut out of? Not that I want to join that business, but just being able to know things, to feel close to him..." She took a clipboard and signed, then handed it back to the guy. "I get to know nothing." She handed her credit card to one of the counter guys.

"You're really going," I said.

"Trust me, I don't want to. I know it looks like me being dependent on my dad, but it's actually me getting out from under his thumb. Setting myself up for med school. If this is how I have to go to school, this is how I do it," she said.

I nodded.

"Do you think Herk was set up?" she asked.

"Yeah," I said.

"You really found a wig hair?" she asked.

I nodded.

"A lot of people wear wigs," she said. "Some of them ride in Dad's car."

I nodded.

"I want to believe him," she said, glancing at the clock. The silence between us got a little awkward. "Most days I do. I don't know. We had an...*honesty crisis* early on." She pulled out the quote fingers for honesty crisis. "Did he tell you?"

I shook my head.

"We patched it up, but now all this shit. He's a good man. I know that."

I nodded. It wasn't my place to argue. But Herk was right—she'd get on that plane and that was it.

Afterwards we hit the Grove, with its endless luxury shops.

At Etro I found a fabulous print gown with a faux-fur-trimmed plunging neckline from a rack.

"A definite do," she said, holding up an emerald green and black dress.

"For you?"

She nodded.

"Do," I said, feeling clever and special for shopping at an Italian luxury design place with the daughter of a mafioso.

She grinned, and we headed back to the changing room.

"I hear you visited Nico," she said over the partition.

"Yeah. We brought him donuts."

"He told me."

"You talked to him?"

"Don't tell Herk," she said. "Herk doesn't like me staying friendly with Nico."

"Nico doesn't want to get back together, though, right?" I asked.

"Fuck no. He's all over Sophia Viga, not that he'll ever get her, but a man can dream. It's cute." She knocked on my dressing room door. "Check it out."

As soon as I had the dress on, I opened the door and looked her over. "Right color, but you need a new bra."

"Weird neckline," she said of mine.

We re-upped on gowns and went back in. I tried on a pink jeweled-bodice gown; she tried a low-back black and white print.

She spun around in the mirror. "Even if he wanted to get back together, Nico would never pull a thing like we're talking about. I mean, the Corvette thing was actually too crafty for him. He'd die if he heard me say that. Nico has a good heart, but he's more of a puppy dog. He follows rules really well. He's great at his job because you can give him instructions and it gets done. Which has its advantages."

"Hot," I said.

"Yeah?" She spun some more.

"Hot as hell."

She pointed at mine. "That's too mother of the bride. Stay there." She left and came back with a pair of red gowns. I closed the door and inspected them. Back when I had red hair I stayed away from red. But hey, it was a new day, and I had platinum hair.

She kept on about Nico. He wasn't entrepreneurial like Herk, she told me. She loved how Herk was a man of vision, how he could see structures where none existed. She told me he was supposed to have gotten some shakedown territory after the wedding and he would've built that territory, whereas Nico would've just ridden it until it dissolved under him. "Of course it doesn't matter now."

I came out in the slinky red gown. Maria clapped her hands. "Fuck yeah!"

We headed out on the quest for accessories, and then we browsed at a sports store and discussed the merits of various yoga mats. Afterwards we split a cinnamon roll at a bench in the shade while her sunglasses-wearing duo of bodyguards sat nearby. That's when it hit me—Nico had said there would be no handing over of territory. *What is this, 1920s Sicily?* he'd said.

I turned to her. "Did Nico not know he was getting territory?"

"We didn't really discuss it. But my sister's new husband got something."

"Did Nico know about that?"

"I don't know. Why?"

"Oh, at Guvvey's last night, he was like, no way would the Don be giving out pieces of his action. Like he knew for a fact that wouldn't ever, ever, ever be happening."

"That's weird," she said.

"Is it weird he'd say that, then?" I asked, thinking maybe I could be getting a new clue for our investigation here.

"Kind of," she said. "Though Nico always wanted people to understand he wasn't with me for the money. It was always really important to him, because people used to say that he was, due to his gambling thing. And it really wasn't true. Nico's a man who falls hard for a woman."

"Do you know what territory Herk would've gotten?" I asked. It probably wasn't that important now that we had our sights set on Kenny James, but my guys were always talking about how every piece of information was important.

"The shit adjoining his central corners up to Oakford Lanes. Dad said he wouldn't feel right running protection under Herk's nose, because it put them at odds." She sighed and looked away. "Herk was so proud to have won him over. He's so into family. His parents are amazing, and the way he takes care of them is amazing."

"He's super into family—I could even see that." And then I

was thinking about Zeus and his white picket fence and family holidays thing.

We hit the bookstore, loading up on way too much awesomeness. I was trying to sell her on a sassy little vampire number when I looked up and found her grinning. She whispered, "Your husbands are here."

I smashed the book into her chest. "Don't let them hear you call them that! God, what am I, a Mormon?"

"Oh, honey, nobody is thinking you're a Mormon."

Odin came up. He grabbed me and kissed me, and then Thor did, and then Zeus did, and I was feeling stupidly happy and Maria was just laughing.

"How'd it go?" I asked.

"We discovered a lot of places where Kenny isn't," Zeus growled. "Fucking Manny James knows where he is, but now we can't find Manny either and..." He ended the sentence with another growl. "You ready to go?"

Maria and I paid for our books while my guys thanked the bodyguards in a very guy way.

My guys and I headed out to the parking lot, weaving between cars. I joked about them having lost their car, which of course would never happen due to their paranoid level of awareness, but the way we were weaving through cars, you'd think it.

I was about to tell the odd little detail about Nico when Zeus tensed and shoved me behind him.

I followed the direction of his gaze to movement in the shadows. Zeus had his piece out. Thor had his piece out. Odin was suddenly nowhere. And then there was more movement out in the shadows, then a grunt and a clunk.

The skirmish turned out to be Odin pressing Noel James's face onto the hood of our Navigator. Noel, the good James brother. Or so we'd thought.

"Fuck!" Noel said.

"What the hell are you up to?" Odin growled.

"I'm not up to anything! I wanted to talk."

Odin pulled a gun from Noel's pocket and let him up.

"You want to talk?" Thor asked.

"Yeah, man—*discreetly*—but I guess I should've hired a skywriter."

"Fine. Come on, then," Zeus said. He clicked the key fob to open the SUV doors. "After you."

"Seriously?" Noel said. "You think I planted a fucking bomb in there?"

"I don't know," Zeus said. "Seems to be the trend."

"Fuck you." Noel yanked open the door and got in, and then Thor and Odin followed him into the back. I got in the front with Zeus.

"Satisfied?" Noel asked.

"Our car was blown up, and it had your brother Kenny's signature all over it," Zeus said. "And Manny didn't want to say where Kenny is, so..."

"I get it, I get it," Noel said.

"You here to give him up?"

"Look," Noel began, "I felt like after your last visit that we were moving toward a better relationship." He nodded at Thor. "I liked working with you. I felt like we had something productive going. You helped my brother."

"How is he?" Thor asked. "Did the swelling dissipate? Are you tracking the color like I told you?"

"Pretty much," Noel said. "He's on the mend, but my brother Manny—you guys, come on, you came into our home uninvited. Now this car bomb shit and you're saying it's Kenny. Manny isn't your bitch, and you can't go at him like you did today."

I looked at my nails, wondering how my guys went at poor Manny today. "People like to be respected," I said.

"Exactly," Noel said.

"And they like their cars not to blow up," Zeus said.

"I get that you're upset by that. I see where it would lead you to think Kenny did it, but I swear to you it wasn't Kenny. We have certain reasons not to want attention put on Kenny, and it has nothing to do with you guys. Manny's pissed off and not in the mood to help you, but you're hurting us with this attention right now. So I'm going to hold out an olive branch and help you and tell you that Kenny is in Bali right now. Bali, as in Indonesia."

"And I'm supposed to take your word for it?" Zeus said.

"You don't have to." Noel pulled out his phone. "Kenny went a bridge too far in the job we pulled, and Manny got him out of the country. Last Friday, it was."

"Must've been quite the bridge too far," Odin said.

Because Indonesia has no extradition treaty with the U.S., I realized.

Noel had Skype open. "I'm reaching out in peace between our families. Manny doesn't know I'm doing this, but this heat from you guys is bullshit, and so is this growing feud. So hopefully you see this and it helps you catch the person who did this. And hopefully it builds up a bit of goodwill between our families." There was a tone and suddenly a voice. "Hey, buddy," Noel said.

"Dude!"

I couldn't see the phone, but Odin and Thor were looking hard.

Noel said, "Do me a favor—go walk onto the porch. I need to see something."

"Like what?" I heard a guy, presumably Kenny, say.

"I need the streetscape. Just go out there and turn around. Just to get the layout. I want to see your neighborhood."

Apparently Kenny did it, and it was convincing—I could tell by the glances that flowed between Zeus and Odin.

"You fucker, look at that sun!" Noel said. "Motherfucker."

"Is Manny there?" Kenny asked.

"Nah. Look, I gotta call you back later." Noel cut the connection.

"That's Bali, alright," Odin said. "Real-time."

"He could've flown down last night," Zeus pointed out.

Noel snorted. "The whole call could've been a film of a film. Look, I'm trying to backchannel here."

Zeus studied his face. I could see him deciding to trust Noel. Finally he nodded. "Okay."

"So you'll back off of Kenny? Yeah, it was his signature with that bomb. Kenny loves a big smoky inferno like that, but I'm telling you it wasn't him. Neither was the Corvette, obviously."

Zeus exchanged glances with Odin. They both bought it.

Odin narrowed his eyes. "Does anybody else know Kenny's in Bali?"

"Just you and us."

"You planning on keeping it that way?" Odin asked.

"Yeah," Noel said. "It doesn't help that you all are asking around about him. The attention is no good."

"Okay, Noel," Zeus said. "No more asking around about Kenny."

"Thanks, man," Noel said.

"Let me ask a favor," Zeus said. "You mind if we let people go on thinking we blame Kenny?"

"You can let people think whatever you like," Noel said. "Let 'em think you found Kenny. Just stop beating the bushes for him, okay?"

"I appreciate it," Zeus said. "I appreciate the cooperation between our groups. And this helps us."

Noel pocketed his phone and took back his piece. "You think you can repair with Manny one of these days?"

"What do you have in mind?"

"Some gesture. Restore the respect."

Zeus nodded. "We'll see."

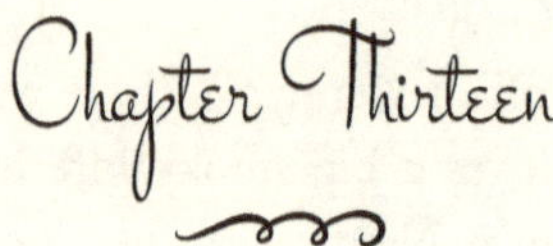

ZEUS DROVE LIKE A MANIAC ACROSS TOWN IN RUSH-
hour traffic. It was partly because we had that reservation for La
Belle in an hour, partly because it made us harder to tail, and partly
because Zeus was Zeus.

My guys were mostly convinced by Noel's story. And while on
the one hand it was good to have a suspect ruled out, it was bad in
another way, because if the bomber wasn't Kenny, who was it?
Danger could come from anywhere.

We were back to square one. Rebels without a clue.
Except not...

"I had an interesting conversation with Maria," I began,
excited to tell the possibly-now-relevant detail about the wedding
gift. "Very interesting."

"That BMW," Thor mumbled, eyes on a passing car.

"It got on at the last entrance," Odin said.

"You sure?" Thor said, and the two of them had a lengthy
exchange that showed how shockingly aware they were of every car
around us.

Fugitive mode. Survival mode. My story could wait until
dinner.

Like a madman, Zeus slid across four lanes of traffic onto an exit.

I had to sit out in the car with Thor while Odin and Zeus did a room-by-room inspection of our posh and fabulous hilltop hideout. Would we even make our reservations? Finally they let me in.

I changed into my gown in less than ten minutes, which my men seriously didn't appreciate enough, being that they were capable of changing their looks in five seconds flat. But they appreciated the result when I strolled out, and that was super-nice.

La Belle turned out to be an old-school, white-tablecloth-and-candles type of place, an institution that was just a little worn around the edges.

We went in and waited at the maître d' stand behind two other couples. Even there my guys were scanning the place, assessing every patron. They fixated on a few people briefly, only to rule them out, all in their silent language of glances and minute movements.

I wrapped my arms around Thor, wearying of the cloak-and-dagger routine.

"This is a hidden gem," Zeus said. "They make a special fish on Valentine's Day, their secret recipe for crab-stuffed sole."

"You've been here?" I asked.

"No," Zeus said mysteriously. "But I've always wanted to come."

And then it was our turn. Zeus told the maître d' that we had a Valentine's reservation for four under Zieman, one of his favorite fake names. The host grabbed menus. "The two couples will dine together?"

"We're one couple," Zeus said. "So yes, we will dine together."

The man looked confused, then he simply led us back.

"Oh, *fucking-g* Jesus," Odin muttered under his breath.

I cringed, remembering the couples massage incident. Thor grinned wickedly.

The host stopped at a pair of window tables. "Together, then," he said, more of a question than anything.

"Push them together, please," I said with a warning look at Zeus.

The man pushed two two-tops together, and we sat. The waiter came with two roses.

"Only one, right in the middle of the table," Zeus said. "We're all together."

The waiter smiled. "Not one for each couple?"

"We aren't two couples," Zeus said. "We—the four of us—are a romantic unit, and we hope to be treated as such."

"Very good," the waiter said diplomatically as he set one bud vase with one rose in it in the center of the table. We ordered our drinks and food.

I exchanged glances with Thor after he left.

"What?" Zeus barked.

"Oh, nothing," I said. "Just sending up a silent prayer that no assholes come around trying to give us more roses."

Odin smiled his glittering smile. "I'm quite sure the news has spread through the entire staff."

"Good," Zeus said. "I'm not ashamed of our relationship. I want everyone to see that we're together."

"I'm proud, too." And at that moment, I was. I reached out and took Odin's hand, and then I took Zeus's hand and I turned and kissed Thor on the cheek. I knew some people thought I was slutty to have three guys, but right then, I couldn't have been more proud.

Odin regarded the rose thoughtfully. I got the feeling he was thinking what I was thinking, how Zeus used to tear those things up.

The waiter delivered our drinks and some little spiced olives and nuts with bread crisps, and my bandits started talking about the case. There was an aliveness to them that I hadn't seen in a long time.

"This is good," Zeus said. "The James Gang thinks we're off Kenny, and everyone else in the world thinks we're on Kenny. Our culprit will relax."

I picked up my glass and swirled around my champagne. "It's too bad you don't have a clever member of the team who knows about the wedding present Maria would have gotten, if only Don Galvano and Herk weren't on the outs. Knows *exactly* what that present would have been."

Three surprised gazes angled toward me, and I enjoyed that feeling.

"She has a dowry after all?" Zeus said.

I smiled. "It's not really a dowry, but yes, territory would have been forthcoming upon the marriage. Though I'm almost considering not revealing all that I learned, being that you sent me dress shopping instead of investigating. Making me feel less than a partner."

"Baby." Zeus gave me his dangerous rangy-bear look. "I am going to start counting."

My belly tightened; I knew what that meant. I sighed and popped a spicy olive into my mouth. "The present would be all of his shakedown territory adjoining his central corners up to Oakford Lanes. The Don felt like he would be stepping on Herk's toes or something, running protection around Herk's corners. Herk won't get that territory now, but it's what he would've gotten if the Corvette thing hadn't happened."

"That's good," Zeus said, and my heart puffed with pride.

"So interesting." Thor pulled out his phone "Why didn't you say anything?"

"I'm sorry that we were busy strong-arming Noel and chasing around and dressing for dinner. I'm telling you now."

He set his phone at the center of the table. It showed a map, and he'd drawn a red square over the territory. "There it is. The territory. Roughly," he said. "Right?"

"So the question is, who would want to prevent that transfer of power?" I said, continuing on my Sherlocky streak.

"Strange," Odin said. "Nico was so sure there was no present. Remember?"

"I thought that was interesting, too," I said. "I asked Maria about it, and she said it was because he always had a complex about seeming to be into her for the money. Nico never wanted people to think he liked Maria only for the money."

Odin raised his brows. "So Nico did know he'd get that territory as a gift?"

"Basically, yeah," I said.

"Nico, Nico, Nico," Odin said, like they'd caught him out.

"What?" I said. "It makes sense to me."

"Not to me. Why would Nico want to pretend to think there is no wedding gift now?" Odin said. "Why would he care? He's whipped on another woman."

I narrowed my eyes.

Odin gave me a delicious look and adjusted his glasses in the sexy way he sometimes did, waiting.

Zeus grunted. "You've learned something interesting, and it's not about the dowry."

Odin paused here and beamed at me while the waiter came to deliver a new round—the cheese platters.

"All very delicious," Odin said, and he wasn't talking about the food.

The waiter smiled and left.

I felt happy and excited now, too. "It's not like Nico's marrying Maria or even with Maria, so why would he make such a point to act ignorant about the wedding present?"

"More precisely, why does he want us to *think* there is no wedding present?" Odin asked. "An why does he want us to believe *he* thinks there is no present?"

I nodded, keeping up, but definitely hoping this was the last twist of the pretzel.

Zeus pulled the phone toward him. "It's weird. Nico has nothing to do with that territory. The Borelli family has no business there. The transfer wouldn't affect him at all. What territory Herk gets should not be interesting to Nico."

"And he's whipped on Sophia Viga and still friendly with Maria," I said. "He has no motive for wrecking that relationship between Herk and Maria or Herk and Don Galvano."

"Nico used Handsome Jack as an alibi," Zeus said. "Maybe we go at it that way. Poke around and see what happens. Maybe there's something there."

"Handsome Jack." Thor takes the phone. "Handsome Jack's isn't in the territory. But he could be..."

"Right. It all depends on how you define *up to Oakford Lanes*," Zeus said. "Does Herk know Handsome Jack? Is there any bad blood there between Herk and Handsome Jack? That would be a motive, if Handsome Jack didn't want Herk in his business."

They all looked at me for some reason.

"What? I'm just a simple sheep farmer."

"Good job, that's all." Zeus slammed his scotch, grabbed his phone from his suit jacket pocket, and beelined out of the restaurant, presumably to call Herk and ask whether he'd had any dealings with Handsome Jack.

"Bottom line, somebody doesn't want that wedding gift to go to Herk," Odin said.

We went over the problem at different angles of thought. It was fun and exciting. But then Odin's expression hardened. I twisted around and saw Zeus strolling across the restaurant in his casual-yet-predatory way, but something was off.

He slid into his chair with a dark look. "Denko is out there."

Odin and Thor straightened.

"Wait—Denko?" I said. "Are you talking about the ZOX agent?"

"Yeah," Odin said. "You sure?"

Zeus nodded gravely.

Hands disappeared under the table. Firearms, I thought with a chill. My pulse raced.

"Pretty sure it was him. He let his hair go gray. It's shorter. He has a crew cut—he looks more straight-laced than when we saw him in Panama. Stern. Steely."

I narrowed my eyes. "Authoritarian and like a statue?" I asked.

"Kind of," he said. "Why?"

"You guys," I said. "*No*. I said I wasn't into it if Zeus wasn't into it."

"What the fuck are you talking about?" Zeus barked, and I could see quite plainly that he wasn't fucking around. And Thor had gone white as a sheet. I heard a click. Somebody checking the chamber.

"ZOX is never a game of any kind," Odin said. "Please know, goddess, that if we are talking about ZOX, there is no chance we are speaking in jest. Or arranging something like with your cartoon girl in the woods."

"Sorry," I whispered, setting down my fork.

"It's okay, baby," Zeus said. "We're okay."

"I don't see anybody in here being off," Odin said. "This is all civilians. Don't you think?"

My guys all agreed. The restaurant was pure civilians.

The waiter set our fish entrées in front of us. They smelled amazing. Buttery, with just a hint of saffron. My heart broke a little because Zeus had so badly wanted this romantic dinner. He wanted this to be like a real Valentine's Day date.

"Eat a little bit, baby," Zeus said. "I wanted you to try it." Something else clicked under the table. A snap. Ankle holster. *Fuck*. "It's stuffed with crab, and they only make it one time a year. There's a delicate hazelnut crust and...I want you to try it. I want to watch you try it."

"Try it, goddess," Odin said.

My heart pounded out of my chest. Everything seemed so final. "What's going to happen?"

"In the next moment," Zeus said, "you are going to enjoy a delicious entrée. And it's going to mean something to us that we could give that to you."

"Stop talking like we're going to die," I said.

"All possibilities exist," Odin said.

"Except Ice dying," Zeus growled.

My eyes teared up so much I couldn't see. "You think you're not going to get away?"

"Of course we *think* we are," Odin said.

"You guys!" I said.

But they were waiting.

With shaking hands, I picked up my fork and pressed the edge into the delicately crusted hunk of fish. I admired it a moment, then slid it between my lips and ate it. Or more like, let it melt in my mouth. "It's delicious," I said. I looked at each one of them. "It really is."

And then my heart did a flip-flop, because that was the end of our dinner.

A long silence followed.

Zeus furrowed his brow. "I don't want to go hot with all these fucking people. All these people having their Valentine's dinner. Fuck if I'm going to shoot up La Belle."

Right then I knew with a kind of weird certainty that La Belle was more than a good place he'd heard of. This place was loaded with some significance.

Thor buried his head in his hands. "Fuck! All the clinic shit is at our house. If they decrypt my laptop, I can never go back down there."

"If they even try to decrypt your laptop it will *fucking-g* combust, my friend."

"Wait, we can't go back to our house?" I said.

Odin turned to me. "Somebody dropped a *fucking-g* dime on

us, Isis. ZOX knows we're in L.A. We have to assume they know where we've been living."

"Or it could be nothing," Zeus said. "A coincidence. But this is how we stay alive. This. Stay light, stay fast."

We'd had a home. A new business. Friends. This wave of grief came over me, for how normal everything had started to seem. And for how badly Zeus had wanted this dinner. "We're alive right now, and I love you guys so much." I put my hand to my heart, because my love for them was so big. "I love you so mind-blowingly much. And you know what? This was one of the best things I've ever eaten. So fuck it." I took another bite of the fish and pointed at them with the tines of my fork. "At least try it."

They all stared at me.

"It's amazing. And we're here. Right now we're here. Two seconds. I want us all to try it. You were right about it being the best ever. And you know what? We found each other by whatever miracle, and we're in this beautiful place in front of this beautiful meal. And we can at least taste it before walking into whatever we're walking into."

Zeus grabbed his fork—with his left hand, of course, being that his right was curled around the grip of a gun under the table. He lopped off a hunk and ate it, closed his eyes as he chewed. Thor and Odin did the same.

"This *is* the best," Thor said.

The waiter came back. "Is everything alright?"

"We just heard of a family emergency." Zeus pulled out a wad of hundreds—twice or maybe three times what it would take to cover our dinners. "And we think there're people out there waiting for us in this sensitive time. You know."

The waiter nodded, thinking paparazzi. Zeus didn't correct him. He put three more hundreds on the table. "Name every exit, including windows."

Odin slid over a napkin upon which he'd already sketched the layout of the place and instructed the waiter to put X's where there were doors and human-sized, operable windows. The waiter hesitated, but then the stack of hundreds grew a bit, and he quickly started writing. He straightened up when he was done. "If I can do anything..."

Zeus said, "Carry on. Lips zipped. The less attention the better."

The waiter, used to dealing with celebrities, though likely celebs he could recognize, nodded crisply. "You want to-go boxes?"

"We can't," I said sadly.

"I'm sorry your dinner had to be interrupted." And then he added, "Happy Valentine's Day to the four of you."

"Thanks, man," Zeus said, clearly grateful for our romantic unit to be recognized.

Odin took off his suit jacket and put it around me. "I'm not cold," I said.

"I know. Grab your purse."

I nodded. This was a time to follow directions unquestioningly. My blood raced.

Zeus said, "Why don't they have eyes in here? Am I crazy?"

"No, this is all civilian," Odin said. "Which is disturbing."

"Let's just focus on leaving," Thor said.

Zeus stabbed at the napkin. "So this is just another bank. But with more exits. Odin, take Isis out through the kitchen. Grab a vehicle. Text when you're coming around." He pointed to another X. "Thor and I get out here."

I nodded and the next thing I knew, Odin was pulling me out of my chair and back across the dining room floor. We pushed through the swinging doors into the kitchen. Once there, he pulled out his gun, pointing it up. "Coming through."

"Hey," somebody said, but then people saw the gun and backed off or raised their hands. Something metal crashed to the floor. It sounded like a pan.

And like that, we were out in the cool night, in a small back parking lot, moving stealthily past two rusted delivery vans and a beater truck. He paused and swore under his breath, then pointed at the street where a black Mercedes four door idled. "There."

"Someone's in it."

"Start your text, but don't hit send."

I complied, entering in black Mercedes.

"Now go get in the back, passenger side."

"Just like that?" I asked.

"Just like that. Hurry."

"What if it's locked?"

"It isn't. He's waiting for somebody. Go!"

I ran around the rail and over the boulevard to where it was parked, and I pulled the back door open. The driver, who had short red hair and a trim beard, twisted around. "What the fuck?"

But then his door opened, and Odin pulled him out of the car and got in. "Send the text." He shoved it into drive and peeled out, jumped the curb, and smashed through the gap in the rail, scraping the shit out of an entire side. He slowed and rolled up the alley that flanked the restaurant. This was the side Thor and Zeus were to come out of. I leaned up into the front and pushed the door, then I opened the back door and scooted behind the driver's seat to make room. Zeus and Thor dove in.

Just at that time, a car appeared in front of us, blocking the way.

"Fuck me." Odin shifted it into reverse and backed up at top speed, smashing past the rail once again. The bearded red-haired man was on the sidewalk, talking on his phone. He put up a hand, like he thought we might shoot him from the car. Or something. He wasn't saying hi, anyway.

Odin jammed the car into drive, and we were off. "Think I fucked up the axle," he grumbled as we pulled into traffic.

"Turn," Zeus said.

He turned. The car was making a grinding sound. We went along tensely. Traffic thickened. Sirens sounded in the distance.

Odin was doing a good job of driving, though Zeus usually had that job. "You're usually the driver," I said to him.

"Logistics," Zeus grumbled.

Logistics? What did that even mean?

It came to me in the next moment that they'd choreographed this escape with me in mind. Of all the zillion combinations ratcheting through my bandits' minds, this one ended up favoring my odds of survival—me fleeing out the back with Odin to protect and drive me, Zeus handling the potential heat inside with help from Thor. It made me feel strange and sad and grateful and insanely in love.

"So far so good," Thor said. About people following, he meant.

"Agreed," Odin said. "Bus station?"

"Take a bus somewhere?" I said.

"Fuck that," Odin said. "If we have to travel by *fucking-g* bus, then ZOX really has won."

I laughed, just out of nervousness.

"We store things there." Thor pulled me to him. "We're okay."

"Does this feel too easy?" Zeus asked after a bit. "Does it feel wrong?" He looked at Odin.

Odin grunted. His meaning was crystal clear: he didn't like it, either. He grunted again. Translation: he really, *really* didn't like it.

We pulled up in the back of the bus station. Zeus strolled in, then came back out with four duffel bags. We got back on the road, with Zeus driving this time.

It turned out they had long-term lockers at the bus station containing go bags, one for each of us. Each was packed with a passport, cash, weapons, wigs, burner phones, and a change of clothes. Odin inspected and destroyed each of our phones.

"This has the feel of Rakan lowlands, Odin," Zeus said.

Odin nodded.

"Dare I ask?" Thor said.

The fact that Thor didn't know about it meant that it was

probably before their time together. When Thor was still a doctor in a relief organization and Thor and Odin were top ZOX spies.

Odin said, "We were assigned to a jungle unit to root out an enemy informant, but the entire unit was the enemy. They'd been killed and replaced. We'd never met them aside from the commander, who they had under their control through threats. So what Zeus meant was, maybe more things are wrong than we think. Maybe it's not just one thing wrong in this picture, Maybe it's the entire picture; maybe it's the frame itself."

"The frame itself? Meaning, the danger surrounds and encloses us? Hangs us on a wall?"

Odin snorted. "More like, ZOX knows who crashed the Corvette. Maybe that's who ratted us out. So they know each clue we will find and follow. They know how we work and where each clue would lead us. They know where we are going, and they knew where we dined. As if we're rats in a maze now, and ZOX is looking down above us, knowing we'll eventually find the center of the maze where our culprit is. Maybe that's why they didn't have eyes on us inside La Belle. They can afford to be loose and lose us, because they know our ultimate destination."

"Using this fucker who ratted us out," Zeus said. "Like bait."

"Except why let us run in the maze at all?" I asked.

"Yes, that is the question," Odin said.

"*One* of the questions," Zeus said. "I have a lot of fucking questions. Maybe it's time to leave the maze."

"And let the motherfucker who ratted us out go?" Thor asked.

"You think I want that any less than you do?" Zeus said.

Odin hissed out an angry breath.

Chapter Fourteen

We resumed a routine I knew well—me in a wig with one of the guys, posing as two lovers who want the best hotel suite in the place.

We couldn't go home again. It got me right in the gut. The little home we'd enjoyed, if only for a matter of months.

This was a hipster hotel, not as posh as we liked, but it was near the airport, and we needed to be able to move out on a dime.

My guys were spooked. They were so rarely spooked. Whenever I asked about it all, they assured me they were being careful, and yeah, I knew they were being careful, but I also knew they were spooked.

Thor and I showed our go-bag passports with our new names and paid in cash that we took out of a congratulations card, putting on our big happy act.

We stepped into the elevator and hit the button for the second floor. The doors slid open, and Thor and Odin came in with their bags, having mysteriously gotten up there while we'd checked in. We rode to the top in silence that was part paranoia, part sadness.

The suite was beautiful—very spare and colorful and modern, and the usual things we loved were there, including a hot tub.

Still, it wasn't home.

"I'll miss that place," I said, meaning our hilltop safehouse.

Zeus got the idea of lending it to the James brothers. "They'd have a lot of use for a place like that once the heat is off us," he said. "Noel really stepped up, and he wants our groups to get along. What do you think?"

We all agreed. Having allies meant everything. It was particularly evident now that somebody had screwed us so bad.

Zeus lowered his bearish bulk onto the couch. "The weather is Paris is shitty right now, but Hong Kong is nice. So is Auckland."

"I can't believe we're actually going," I said.

"It's time. ZOX got too close," Zeus said.

"We flew too close to the sun." Odin stared out the window, weary and unhappy.

I wrapped my arms around my middle. My guys never gave up. This Agent Denko really had spooked them. And poor Herk and Maria.

Odin said, "We could do a pit stop in Honolulu if we went east. Re-up on go bags."

"You have go bags in Honolulu?"

"My favorite identity is there," he said.

"There's always Jerba," I said. That was the island in Tunis I always wanted us to go to.

Odin groaned. "An old man's place to fish."

"Tokyo has that place with the hot tub that feels like you're in a grotto," Thor said. "Isis would enjoy that hot tub very much."

I went and put my arms around him. "Do they give you fluffy bathrobes?"

Thor brushed back the hair from my forehead. "Would we take you to a place that doesn't have fluffy bathrobes? Would we do that, baby? What would we wrap you up in after we fuck your brains out?"

"Yeah," I said. "I accept only the fluffiest of robes after my brains are fucked out. No terrycloth for me!"

Odin got on the burner phone to look at flights. "They'll be looking international."

Thor said, "Honolulu would be nice."

Odin found a set of flights. He decided he and Thor could go separately, routing through San Francisco, and I'd go with Zeus. Nothing we wanted left until the morning. Eight hours.

We bought the tickets.

"So we relax for eight hours," Zeus said, looking me up and down, and then he looked out the window, out at the city lights, too upset to fuck. We all were. Everything was wrong.

I joined him at the window and gazed down at the crosshatch of roads outlining big box stores with their blocky rooftops. Thor and Odin came over, and we all just stood there, not saying anything.

"Except somebody fucking *dropped a dime* on us," Zeus said finally.

The silence turned to chill.

"Think about it," Zeus continued. "On *us*. I'm gonna be honest, when Galvano was saying that shit, I thought, 'Nobody's going to drop a dime on us.'"

"And somebody went and did," Thor said.

"They assumed ZOX would take us out," Odin said. "Before we got to him."

"Ratted us out," Zeus spat.

"It's whoever crashed that Corvette," Thor added.

"Oh, definitely." Zeus grabbed a bottle of scotch from the wet bar. "Somebody ratted on us. I can't tell you how good it would feel to just—"

"To sink our fangs into his flesh as we viciously rip him apart. Tear him into little bits of fiery pain that swirl into the bowels of hell," Odin said.

Probably not how Zeus meant to finish it, but it worked.

"It would feel good," Thor agreed.

"Except, hello, if we solve the mystery, that would lead us straight to ZOX. It's the one place ZOX knows we'll go," I said.

Silence. I wasn't liking that silence.

"Right?" I said. "Amirite?"

Zeus studied the bottle.

Gulp.

"You guys. We can't."

"They dropped a dime on us, Ice!" Zeus growled. "And what about Herk? We let somebody wreck his and Maria's life? This life they could've had?"

"Right," I said. "And I want to sink my teeth into this person's jugular and rip them like a satanic tiger snake blowtorch, too, and I'm not even a tiger-snake-blowtorch type of person. I get it. It's bullshit."

"Total bullshit." Zeus topped off his drink. "That's why I'm using the next eight hours to solve this mystery and kick some ass."

"Fuck yeah, brother," Odin said.

"Wait, *what?*"

Zeus took a swig and wiped his mouth with the back of his hand. "God, I feel better already. For a minute there I was in danger of not being able to look myself in the mirror ever again."

"Me either," Odin said.

"Wait, what about the maze? Us as rats? The evil picture frame?"

"Fuck it," Odin said.

Thor pulled out his phone. "We need to think a little bit more about that territory Galvano was handing over. That's the key."

"Agreed," Odin said.

"No, timeout!" I said.

"We're fine." Zeus passed the bottle to Odin. "We go back and clear it up in time to get out of town. It's something they won't expect. Thor, you and Ice hold down the fort while we have a chat with the Don."

"Wait, no," Thor said. "I want in."

"Who's going to protect Ice?"

"Fuck you," I said, getting off Thor's lap and grabbing the bottle from Zeus. "We're a family. If we're foolish, we're foolish together."

Chapter Fifteen

ZEUS SET UP ANOTHER MEETING WITH DON GALVANO, this one in a trendy comfort-food diner off the hotel strip, prized for its darkness.

We all used our change of clothes from the go bags. They'd packed a sweet little black pantsuit with a pink top and fabulous boots for me. It had Thor's taste written all over it. I put it on and smiled at him. He came over and adjusted my lapels. My bandits wore nice shirts and ties. The guiding principle of go-bag clothes was that they needed to be flexible enough for dressing down or dressing up, because you never knew what circumstance they'd be used in.

We were hungry for food and for answers by the time we arrived, being that we'd never gotten to eat our beautiful meal. I ordered stuffing and mashed potatoes. The guys got burgers.

Galvano came in with his bodyguard, who lingered at the bar while the Don slid in next to Odin.

"Don't you know it's Valentine's Day?" Galvano said. "You oughta feed your little lady something nicer."

Thor's lips quirked. "We feed her lots of nice things."

I felt my cheeks flame red. I kicked him under the table.

Odin passed Galvano a map of Los Angeles. "We have reason to believe the Corvette crash is linked to the wedding gift you were planning on giving Herk."

"He's not getting it anymore," Don Galvano said.

"Right," Zeus said, stuffing a fry into his mouth. "We suspect that was the desired result of crashing the Corvette, to get you mad at Herk. Somebody didn't want that territory to get turned over to Herk."

"Barely anyone knew it would happen," he said. "Maria, my lawyer, Stan doing the collections."

"What about your lawyer and Stan? Would either of them have a problem with it?"

"No way," Galvano said. "Stan was going to get a promotion. Lawyer gets paid either way. Maria...she wouldn't do anything to nix it."

Zeus asked him to mark the exact territory. Galvano drew a careful square around the part he'd aimed to give. He took off soon after.

Zeus pointed at the map. "Can't help but notice that Handsome Jack's is in here."

"Could be a coincidence," Thor said. "Handsome Jack is into everything."

"But Nico lied about the wedding gift—he specifically wanted us to think there was no gift of territory, or at least that he thought there was none, and Handsome Jack is his alibi," Zeus said. "These connections mean something. We just don't see what yet."

They formulated a plan. Zeus would speak with Stan and see whether Stan told anybody. I was to return to the room with Thor and Odin and call Maria to see whether she told anybody else. Then we'd head to Handsome Jack's.

We paid and left before dessert had arrived. Zeus dropped us off at the hotel while he went to visit Stan. We used our key cards to go in the side door and headed into the stairway, but I stopped them. "Wait."

"What?"

"I need something chocolaty."

"We'll send up."

"But all they ever have is fancy cake stuff in room service." I dug in my purse and found a buck. "My needs are simple. A Kit Kat. I saw one in the machines out..." I pointed at the pool area with a beseeching glance.

"Fuck if we're walking through that lobby together," Odin said.

"We'll go out the side," I said. "Would that be more prudent?"

Odin sighed.

"Chocolate and wafers..."

Odin rolled his eyes. "Come on." He led us down into the basement through an employees-only door.

"You couldn't find a freakier route than this?" I joked. "We could scale down from the roof disguised as tiger snake devil blow-torches."

He grabbed my hair, and in a growly voice, he said, "And after you have your dessert, we will consume ours—slowly and thoroughly. Can you guess what our dessert will be?"

"Umm...my tears of utter pleasure?"

He tightened his grip on my hair, and a wild thrill shot through me. I was crazy with adrenaline, and suddenly all I could think of was fucking. He yanked again, pulling me up to his face, so that our lips were a hair's distance from each other. "Close enough."

"Okay," I breathed.

He pushed me onward on our freakily circuitous route out to the machine by the pool, which was closed. But a hotel pool area was no match for my kinky bank robbers. Odin picked the lock and let me in.

Thor went with me to the bright, beckoning machine while Odin continued on to the gate that ran along the street. The gate had that plastic-type stuff woven into it to create a sheen of privacy.

"You want anyth—"

I didn't finish the word due to Thor's hand clapping over my mouth. Odin was speeding toward us, silently and smoothly, gun down at his thigh, and when I angled my eyes up, I saw Thor had his out, pointing upward.

Odin pointed at me, and then down, which meant stay. I nodded.

He and Thor headed to the gate and crouched down, watching. I stuffed my buck in my pocket and clutched my purse, making myself small against the wall like they'd taught me.

Thor came back past me like I wasn't even there and disappeared back into the hotel. This was full-on secret-agent mode.

Odin was picking the lock on that side. When he finished, he put a finger to his lips and beckoned me over.

I snuck over and crouched next to him. He put his lips to my ear and whispered, "The red sedan is ZOX. I made them when one of them stepped out. Watch us take this motherfucker down, baby."

My heart pounded.

A car slid up from the far corner. "That's Thor," he whispered. "You stay crouched until we signal, and then you get the fuck into the driver's seat. You drive."

I nodded.

Thor had made his usual muscle-car selection—a souped-up Mustang with a blower in front. It was a car made for speed, a car made for chases, a car made for getting laid by hot girls in the most cherished fantasies of teenaged boys. My heart melted a little.

I swallowed as Odin slipped through the now-open gate door, moving fluidly across the street and then up along a row of parked cars and up to the ZOX car.

Was that Agent Denko in there? It was too dark out to see inside his car.

Odin slammed his gun into the window, breaking it. I could see movement in there as Odin pulled the door open. A chaos of hands.

In a flash Odin was hauling the man out.

Agent Denko.

Thor zoomed up, got out, and ran around to help Odin.

My blood raced. I'd never seen Agent Denko in person, but his image was burned into my mind from my guys constantly showing me photos of him—they wanted me to be able to recognize him if I ever saw him. We even had a few photos of him up on our refrigerator.

And here he was. Agent Denko of ZOX.

Maybe it was because I'd stared at his picture so often, but he seemed mythical, somehow. Larger than life.

Like looking at Mickey Mouse stuff and then you go to Disney World and actually meet Mickey Mouse, and suddenly you're face to face with this actual giant mouse with a massive smiling face and three-fingered hands.

Except Denko was way more frightening.

Chapter Sixteen

ODIN PULLED DENKO INTO THE BACK WITH HIM, GIVING
him all kinds of not-fucking-around orders like *Fingers laced on top
of your head!* and *Don't you fucking-g move a muscle.* He promised
to *fucking-g* end him in some painful and colorful ways.

Thor got out and waved me around into the driver's seat.

I scurried across and slid in. Thor went over to Denko's car.
He flicked out a switchblade, blond hair swinging, and bent over,
ruthlessly jabbing the thing into the tire.

I was used to seeing Zeus and Odin be destructive, but there
was something particularly exquisite about Thor, with his beautiful teen-idol looks, playing the gutter dog. He straightened up
and beelined back, eyeing me steadily. And maybe I was an irrevo-
cably depraved person by this point, especially considering that
Odin had the most dangerous individual possible right there in the
back seat, but I was looking at Thor thinking, *We are so going to
fuck tonight.*

Thor slammed into the passenger seat. "Go, go, go!"

I peeled out in first, beating the thing a little, then quickly
shifted to second. Growing up on a farm, you start driving a stick

shift early and often. My driving freed up Odin and Thor to concentrate on Denko.

"Keep straight. Ten blocks," Thor said calmly, holding his silver Sig where Denko could see it, letting it rest all casual and badass in a way that might increase his hotness, were a person depraved in that way. "Then turn on Suncrest."

I glanced in the rearview, taking a good look at the agent who had been following my guys for so long, part of the organization that was responsible for so much of their misery. Our misery.

He had a salt-and-pepper crew cut, a pleasant diamond-shaped face, and nice eyes, which he currently held in a kind of movie-star-style squint, though I was guessing he was more doing that out of pain than out of any attempt to look like Brad Pitt. A cut on his lip bled into the gray scruff of his chin. He was maybe forty.

"You don't get to look at her—not even in a mirror," Odin said.

Denko cast his gaze downward.

"I'm going to take your phone and the rest of your weapons," Odin said. "If you try to stop me, one of us will shoot you in the head, and then we'll take your stuff. A lot easier, but we don't want your brains all over the car, and certainly not on Isis's pretty hair. I mean, can you blame us?"

Denko glanced darkly at the seat in front of him, but said nothing about my pretty hair.

Odin got busy taking things from the man's pockets and elsewhere. I couldn't see much, and it was probably a good thing. I needed to concentrate on the road. Five blocks to the turn.

A stolen car and a hostage. *We had a hostage.*

Odin scrolled through Denko's phone. "This is one way to solve mysteries. Just put out the word that we're on the case and see who fucking turns us in to ZOX."

"You won't get anything off of there," Denko said.

Odin opened the window and threw it out. "Will I get anything out of you?"

"Will you?" Denko asked. "It's one of your specialties, Rashad."

I stiffened. *Rashad?* That was Odin's name? I'd never known his name.

When they first took me hostage, my guys didn't tell me their names, not wanting to put me in additional danger. And then the weeks turned into months, and I made the choice never to ask. It was a gesture of faith in our life, in our future. I'd wanted to know about their pasts, but I was more interested in our future than the demons of their past.

And here one was, in the back seat of the car.

Rashad. I rolled his name around in my mind. It was a beautiful name. I wanted to tell him that, but not in front of Agent Denko.

"You could get a mother to give up her own baby," Denko continued, "isn't that what they always said?"

"You really want to be talking to me like that?" I glanced back in time to see Odin's hand tightening around Denko's neck. "Do you?"

"Do you still have the nightmares?" Denko's voice was getting strained. "Do you think you'll really get something out of me?"

I blinked at the road, feeling like my own air was getting choked off.

He won't kill him, I told myself. My guys weren't killers.

Except for the stalker I'd had a few months back. And they'd killed as agents. They'd kill to protect me. To protect each other.

Denko's voice became a high, strained whisper. "You really think you could?"

The next thing I heard was Denko sucking in a huge gulp of air, and then coughing. "Probably not," Odin said.

"I'm flattered, Rashad."

I concentrated on my driving, ignoring the tension in the car.

"Do you know what the most painful bone to have broken in the body is?" Odin asked him.

"I don't," Denko said.

"Use my name again and you'll find out."

Denko sniffed. "You don't like me using your name? We know all of your names. Except Isis. But we're close. We'll get it, Isis. You think we won't? You think whoever you're protecting is safe—"

Crack.

I didn't need to glance back to know the man was out cold.

"Take a right up here," Thor said, glancing between me and the back seat.

"Damn," I said, taking the turn.

"You're okay," Odin said, texting somebody—Zeus, probably. "We're all okay."

"Go all the way up to that light," Thor said. "The motel's just beyond that strip mall." He twisted back to Odin. "What do you think?"

Denko groaned. Rousing.

"Good enough," Odin said. They discussed what do to with the car.

"Mero Inn," Denko said. "A little below your standards, isn't it?"

Thor ignored him. "Pull in here."

I heard another grunt from the back. I glanced back to see Denko gagged and blindfolded. Odin was texting. Who was he texting at a time like this? Just then Thor's phone pinged. Thor pulled it out, then showed it to me.

WE'RE BUGGED, MAYBE TRACKED.

I nodded to show I understood. Thor took off his shoes and his belt and pointed at my shoes and my purse. I handed them over. He passed the stuff back to Odin.

When I looked back next, Odin was holding up my purse strap for us to see—there was a small metal doodad right above the buckle.

"Let's get a room," Odin said. "We'll wait for Zeus here." He got out and shut the door a few times—to represent the group of us getting out?—and then walked across the parking lot to a dumpster and threw the strap in. He got back in and stabbed a finger at the road...and it wasn't the road he was mad at.

It was bad that my purse had been listening to every conversation.

Very bad.

When had ZOX gotten to my purse? I thought of all the times we'd gone out to eat. Sometimes I put my purse under my seat. Could they have gotten it one of those times? I thought about the breakfast place we'd gone to before meeting Herk. We'd sat at the counter. Some guy had leaned in to grab the ketchup and jostled my purse. Enough that I'd looked inside after to ensure my wallet and phone were still there.

Shit.

Could they have been listening all that time?

I drove us out of there. Thor put his finger to his lips and wrote another text, this one for me to read—*we're going to the Gigis'. Could be other transmitters.*

The Gigis lived in a blue bungalow in Echo Park. The street was dark, but their home was instantly lit with floodlights the second I turned in. I'd only been there twice, but both times had been memorable events. One was Angel's thirtieth birthday bash, a kind of crazy girls-only party. The other was a holiday-card-making party where we personalized a lot of the cards for the various mobsters and thieves in our set. It was thoughtful of them—when you're a criminal with no known address, you aren't getting any holiday cards.

Thor made a finger looping signal for me to pull around the back and park.

Odin stayed in the car with our prisoner while Thor and I headed up to the back door together. Macy emerged in sleek pants and sleek strappy top, almost like a yoga outfit. She had a wand in her hand and a dark look on her face.

So they'd texted ahead.

She motioned for me to hold out my arms. I complied, and she waved it all over my body, and then she did Thor and the bag part of my purse.

"You're clean." She spoke in low tones. "This baby would've sounded off on any kind of transmitter or GPS, and I don't care if it's ZOX-issue or what."

"Would it get something subdermal?"

She cast a dark gaze at the car, clearly not loving that we had a hostage.

"He's blindfolded," Thor said. "He doesn't know where he is."

"And what if he has a subdermal?"

"Don't worry," Thor said, "we'll get him out of here."

Macy handed him the wand. "I'm not involved. You lay him out and do him just for metal." She showed Thor the settings on the thing. "Hold it an inch above. Get the covering surface to line up." She demonstrated on me, then handed it over with a shake of her head. "And keep that motherfucker blindfolded."

Macy and I watched Thor head back to the car. She shook her head and snorted as Odin and Thor pulled Agent Denko out and laid him down. "And here I thought the takeover robberies were the ultimate death wish."

"We'll be okay."

She raised one eyebrow. "You think? Why, because your guys are so high-performance, so high-functioning? The *fucking-g* most badass *fucking-g* robbers?" she said, mimicking Odin. "Shit."

Jenny came out just then. "Hey Ice," she said sleepily. "What's up?"

"Oh, just the God Pack deciding to drive one of their most dangerous and high-value hostages to our place."

Jenny widened her eyes at me—a look of surprise, but a little bit of an impressed look, like, *this is soooo badass.*

I smiled uncertainly, like, *thanks?*

Macy nodded at the car. "Give these boys some duct tape. Not the pink stuff. And no prints. Use gloves and pull off the top layer first, for fuck's sake."

"Got it." Jenny headed in.

"He's under control," I said.

"Really? 'Cause you know what I'm seeing when I look at this scene? It's like those guys who put up ramps and jump their car over a whole lot of other cars, and your guys with their bank takeovers, they can jump ten fucking cars, all lined up in a row— just barely, but they can do it, and it's super-ballsy and yeah, everyone's impressed. But this whole investigations bit? This here is car number eleven."

I thought about how happy they'd been, chasing those clues. Helping Herk. Defying all good sense. A fuck-you to the world. Was that why Zeus had wanted to do the P.I. business so bad? Just to push it?

"Well, you always have a place here," she said. "Unless you drag some federal agent-turned-hostage along. You want to do that, you ca find another pajama party."

"We're good."

We watched them truss the agent up under the watchful eyes of Jenny, who was pointing out places they needed more duct tape.

"He knows all their real names," I added. "I kind of hate that he knows them and the way he uses them, sort of like weapons."

"Enemies. What're you going to do?"

I thought about what Denko had said about Odin having nightmares. It made me realize Odin never actually slept through the night in my bed. Was that because of nightmares? And how could I not know a thing like that? Should I have pushed for their names? Their histories? "I didn't even know their names."

"Don't let this guy fuck you up," she said. "He's got nothing a little duct tape over the mouth won't fix."

Macy, as it turned out, really was on her way to yoga—

midnight yoga. Because apparently the Gigis had to be endlessly fabulous in every possible way.

Thor had come up to where we were, and he jokingly offered to drop her off. "You could squeeze in next to our guest, I'm sure he wouldn't mind."

She gave him the kind of long, dirty look that only she could pull off.

He got serious after that and asked her to let Noel James know that my purse had been listening to every conversation I'd had over the past few days. "It's probably nothing—ZOX wants nothing to do with police investigations—but they should be aware."

We headed off to a new hotel, still with me driving, all the better to free up my men for holding guns on Agent Denko. Even with his duct-tape bindings, gag, and blindfold, they stayed hyperalert.

"Can you think of any time you were separated from your purse?" Thor asked.

"Remember when we stopped for breakfast before meeting Herk?" I said. I reminded them of the guy who'd come up to grab ketchup. We'd all marked him.

"Goddamn," Odin said. "That's what he was up to."

"So they've had ears since then," Odin said.

"What the fuck," Thor grumbled.

Odin had me take a completely bonkers route to the next hotel, a sort of curlicue of turning this way and that, presumably so Denko couldn't estimate the distance and direction. I pulled up in front of an Asian-themed hotel on Hill Street.

"You two do the check-in," Odin said softly. "First floor, end if possible."

We went in for the second time that night as the young married couple. We wrote down a fictitious car and license plate, and luckily the desk clerk wasn't in the mood to confirm that.

I stopped Thor outside the lobby entrance. Just us two, out in the night, full of adrenaline. Even the stars in the sky above seemed brighter and wilder somehow. "What are you going to do with him? Are you gonna..."

I didn't say *kill*.

I didn't need to.

"Only if we have to," Thor said. "I mean, if it's a matter of us or him, that's one thing, but I don't think it'll come to that. Part of our point to these fuckers is that we're not the killers that they are."

"Because of what you saw way back when," I said.

"Yeah, and you don't know about that. You shouldn't even know that much."

"I want to know. I'm in this with you. I should know. It's not because I don't care that I don't ask."

"I know, baby."

"So we keep him as a hostage?"

"As long as we need him. Then we'll pack him off somewhere. Maybe in the back of a freighter going to Omaha or something. Or put him in an abandoned building and call in his location once we're safe elsewhere."

"Safe elsewhere...like in Jerba?"

Thor furrowed his brow. "You think a little setback like this will send us to a boring vacation paradise? Please."

Playfully, I hauled off to hit him and he caught my arm and kissed me, a deep, hard kiss that had all the excitement of the night built into it.

And oh my god, I shouldn't have been horny, but I was.

A few minutes later, the three of us were in the hotel room, all of us sitting on one queen bed with Denko bound up on the other.

Chapter Seventeen

Denko's hands and feet were encircled with silver duct tape, and he himself was bound to the headboard, right around the chest, but at least his blindfold was off.

He kept mumbling, wanting to talk. Thor and Odin had already let him pee, so it couldn't be that.

And he was glaring at us. Hard.

Mumble mumble. All urgent.

"I don't *fucking-g* think so," Odin said, scrolling through his phone investigating bus routes. Eventually he found a route that was running at two in the morning going past us with the right timing. He sent Thor to dump the Mustang and bus it back.

Odin let me pick a TV show. I went for a *Silver Spoons* rerun. The TV equivalent of comfort food. He didn't say anything against it. Partly to indulge me and partly because Agent Denko had appeared extremely unhappy with my choice.

Odin pulled off his jacket and shirt and hung them up nicely. You could see part of his tattoo poking out under his T-shirt. Our tattoo—*You WISH we were dead, motherfuckers.* I wondered whether Denko knew about it. It was odd to think it was a message to him and his people, in a lot of ways. Though it was more a message to anybody in the world who would ever oppose us.

I threw him my fine suit jacket and he hung that up, too. My filmy, silk tank top was a bit sheer, but Odin didn't seem to mind, and I sure the hell didn't. And then Odin and I sat in our bed and watched TV, nestled close. It felt good to have skin-to-skin contact with him. I felt like we were a unit against Denko, like as long as we were touching, nothing could hurt us.

When the show got extra boring, Odin took off his glasses and kissed my hair, leaving his mouth on my head, making a circle of warmth, like a warm link between us, his gorgeous lips, his strong soft arms.

I tipped my head over to look at steely, stern Agent Denko. Odin put a hand on my forehead and tipped my head back. "Don't look at him," he said. "He is nothing to us and nothing against us."

Another episode of *Silver Spoons* began, but it wasn't very calming; I'd never felt more wired, every nerve on a knife edge.

We were on our second *Silver Spoons* episode by the time Thor got back.

He put a plastic grocery bag on the dresser and got right into bed on the other side of me and pulled up the covers over us.

"Zeus isn't back yet?"

"He just checked in," Odin said. "Running a few things down."

"One thing I don't get," I whispered. "I thought they wanted to kill you guys. If they had my purse bugged and were following us, they could've taken us down at any time."

Odin kissed me. "They don't have anything on you. They wanted something on you." He spoke at a normal volume. Like he didn't give a fuck if Denko heard.

"So they could arrest me, too?" I asked.

Odin got this sad, wistful look. "That would be merely secondary, goddess."

I widened my eyes. I'd seen enough cop shows to know the

answer to this. "Because they thought they could flip me? Make me tell things about all of you in exchange for a deal." I leaned forward and glared past Odin clear to Denko. "We are a family. You think I'd ever tell something that would hurt my men in any way? The fuck I would *ever*!"

Denko's expression was unreadable. Of course. Probably a prerequisite for a law man, the unreadable expression.

But I needed him to hear me, needed him to understand that I'd go down with my guys to the end. "It would never happen!" I sat back in a huff, heart thundering.

"It's not that, goddess," Thor said from the other side of me. "Not quite that, much as we appreciate the sentiment."

"Then what?"

Odin took a lock of my hair and twirled it around in his finger, shiny platinum against golden brown. "My guess: they thought if they got something on you—some evidence that would end with you doing hard time—that they could use it for leverage on us. They imagined..." he turned his head away from me, toward Denko, "I am guessing they imagined that we would be willing to turn ourselves in without a firefight if we thought it could get you a deal. Something like that."

I placed my hands on Odin's beautiful whiskery cheek and turned his head back to me. "Is it true?"

"What do you think?"

Yes.

Shivers sailed through me as I stared into the depths of his amber eyes. There were no words, only the wild and untamed love I had for these men, for this family of ours. "I couldn't live with that. We go down together."

"Do not quarrel, goddess," Odin said. "In any case, you would have no choice."

"I wouldn't let you make a deal. I would bring myself down first."

"Nobody's fucking going down," Thor said from the other

side. "Do we look like we're going down?"

"True," Odin said. "We won't go down." In a slightly huskier voice he added, "At least not metaphorically. There are other ways I would gladly go down."

I gasped softly.

Odin kissed me then, taking my lips roughly, hand heavy on the side of my neck. Then he slid his hand down heavily, down down down, trailing kisses as he went, approaching my breast.

"Odin!" I whispered. "Denko."

"What's he going to do? Arrest us?"

He pushed me against the headboard, kissing me harder.

I closed my eyes, blissing out at the rough contact. I felt Thor take my lips, then felt his hand land on my belly.

Agent Denko mumbled, but he didn't matter anymore.

Thor pulled away. "Whatever you say, Denko."

I opened my eyes and smiled into Thor's beautiful blue gaze, crazy with love and unbridled energy, and it was so insane, us in one bed and Agent Denko in another.

Unlike Maria, I really did believe that in the caveman days, women chose mates based on which guy could beat up the other guys, and that was definitely the case in some of my very favorite books. And right now it was ultra-hot that Odin and Thor were utterly in control of this seriously scary guy.

I probably shouldn't have been turned on by it.

A ding from Odin's phone. Zeus. Without taking his arm from around my shoulders, Odin texted back and forth with Zeus in some kind of code. I stayed against him, enjoying the way his steely arm muscles fired with his texting movements, enjoying Thor's hand on my belly, his breath against my neck.

How could he be so casual about it? Personally, I had a 24-hour news crawl of pure exclamation marks looping though my lizard brain. And then there was inappropriate sexual excitement, with more exclamation marks.

Odin put away his phone. "He'll be a while. He's following the gossip grapevine, which, as you know, is quite thriving in our community."

It was true—the gossip among the criminal set made *The Real Housewives of New Jersey* look like monks on seven-year vows of silence.

"We're taking whoever did this so fucking down," Odin said. "And then we'll go somewhere *fucking-g* amazing."

"Yeah," I said, heart pounding, breathing in Odin's warm man scent. Was it possible men gave off extra pheromones from the act of having dominated a lesser man?

Just a question.

No reason.

"This is cozy," Thor said. "Don't you think it's cozy, Agent Denko?"

Denko turned his head to stare. I got the feeling he was trying to look confident. Or maybe he was confident.

"Don't *fucking-g* address him," Odin said.

"Why not?" Thor asked. "It's a free country. Isn't that right, Denko? Oh, no, you say? Not if you know too much? Then it's not? Is that what you're saying?"

Odin reached over my head and bopped Thor's forehead.

Another episode of *Silver Spoons* started up, leading us to discuss who the fuck of the subset of people up at two in the morning would ever watch it. Maybe it was there for all of the wrongdoers of the world to take comfort in after a hard day of violence.

"Any requests, Denko?" Thor asked.

"Do not engage him," Odin said.

"But he looks so stern," Thor said, and I could hear this smile in his voice. That was never a good sign. "Isis, doesn't he look *stern?*"

Chapter Eighteen

"I'm not engaging him," I said, nestling into Odin's shoulder, glad Odin was on the side between us and the agent. "Fuck that."

"You should look at him," Thor said. "He has a certain gravity, don't you think? So stern and disapproving."

I sat up with my mouth hanging open. "Oh my god." Because I got it then—he was talking about my type to watch.

Thor slid a warm hand onto my thigh under the covers. "Look over at him," he whispered.

"Fuck you," I laughed.

"Thor," Odin said...but there was a certain huskiness to his voice.

In his rumbly, velvety voice that always turned me on, Thor said, "Denko is stern and very statue like with a lot of *gravitas*, wouldn't you say, goddess? And very disapproving. In fact..." He moved his hand an inch up my thigh and lowered his voice, "I don't think I've ever known anybody to be quite so disapproving of us as Denko. I mean, it's his life goal to bring us down."

"That *is* a sign of disapproval," Odin said.

I gasped softly as Thor inched his hand up my thigh some more.

"You can't get more disapproving than that," Thor continued in that sexy voice of his where he managed to be both velvety and gravelly. "Or authoritarian. What do you think, Odin?"

I looked over to meet Odin's smoldering look.

"Have you both gone insane?" I said.

Thor brought his hand up nearer to the cleft between my legs. My heartbeat thundered.

"I ask you," Thor continued, "can you be more authoritarian than to belong to an organization more powerful and more secretive than the CIA? But with way more badass initials, of course. ZOX. How can CIA compete? Come on, Ice, look at him."

I looked over to see him still glaring. Yes, he was stern and authoritarian. He was disapproving, clean cut. A little bit dangerous, but utterly under the control of my men. And tied up...and super-stern. So stern.

I clunked my head back against he headboard. "You guys."

But of course, it was a fantasy of mine. And they knew it. And the fact that they knew it gave them a strange kind of control over me. Naturally, this was hot, too. The whole thing was a hotness party.

In a low rumbly voice, Odin said, "He does not like it when we talk about his agency. He wonders how many people know. Worries how to contain this information. Always wants to contain information. We spit on him," he said. "We spit on him and all that he stands for." Here Odin raised his voice, addressing Denko without bothering even to look at him. "You are dirt to us." And then he kissed me full on the lips—a hot, possessing kiss. And at that moment Thor touched a finger between my legs.

"Oh my god," I breathed, nearly twisting up with the sheer pleasure of it. "We can't." "Why not, goddess?" Thor said. "Is it not like what you imagined?"

Odin whispered into my ear, "You love this. I can see it in your eyes. You have never met a thrill you do not like, baby."

Thor took hold of my hair and turned my head to him again. "Do you feel his eyes on us?" He brought his lips to my ear, tickling the shell. "Do you feel the gravity of his gaze?" With a smile in his voice he added, "Do you feel it on your skin? Remember how you told us about that feeling that you love? Up on the top of a ski jump—one push and then gravity takes you? Isn't this like that? Our stern, dangerous enemy. Tell me you don't want to fuck right now. Because I very much do. I want to take you in front of him. We will never find a man sterner. Certainly not more unwilling."

"Not without taking more hostages, anyway."

I closed my eyes. The combination of adrenaline and lust was like a drug. "Yeah, but..." I was thinking about Zeus.

"Feel his eyes on your body," Odin said. "He doesn't want to watch but he will not be able to help himself, because we are so *fucking-g* badass together."

"What about Zeus?" I said. "He's so against this."

"We're outlaws," Odin growled. "The last time I Googled outlaw, it said we do whatever we please and nobody gets to stop us. Nobody tells us no. Zeus doesn't get to make up new rules, and he knows it."

"You're an outlaw, Ice," Thor whispered. "We're all outlaws. Let's be fucked up together."

"I want to be fucked up," I said. "I do."

Odin rose up from where he was and went around to the foot of the bed and pulled off the covers. Then he grabbed my ankles and pulled me down so that I was laying flat on my back.

I loved Denko's eyes on us—I did. The stern, dark watcher. It heightened everything so much.

Thor crawled over me and kissed me. "There we go, goddess." He thumbed my cheek, taking my lips in his. It was so forbidden and so thrillingly wrong, for a minute I wanted to sink into him, into his everything.

Then I stopped. I pressed my hands to either side of Thor's cheeks and pushed away his face. "This will seem like cheating to Zeus," I said.

"Zeus will get over it," Odin said from where he was about to do god knows what with my feet or maybe legs. "You can't change the rules in the middle of the chess game."

"But still..." I said.

"You don't want to?" Thor asked. "You're sure?"

"I'm sure," I said. "We just can't."

Thor sighed and flopped over by my side. "Okay."

"You're sure?" Odin said.

"I'm sure I want to, but I can't not think of Zeus."

"We may need to teach you outlaw lessons." Odin went over to the dresser where Thor had deposited his bag of waters. He twisted the cap off one of them. "I respect that, Ice. We will not fuck in front of Denko, then. I would offer for us to fuck you in the shower, but it seems imprudent to leave our guest alone."

"Oh well," I said.

Denko began to grunt from under the duct tape gag, shifting around, rocking the headboard he was tied to like something urgent was up.

"Fuck off," Thor said.

Odin frowned. "We've had him a few hours. We could see what the fuck. Give him water."

Thor nodded. "I guess."

Odin went over. "You yell or scream, and I will tape your entire *fucking-g* face, got it? I will give you a duct tape mummy head with nostril holes and that's it. You understand?"

Denko nodded.

I cringed as Odin picked up a corner of the tape with a fingernail. When he had a grabbable bit, he just ripped it right off.

Ouch.

Denko grunted and licked his lips.

"What?" Odin asked. "What's so fucking urgent?"

"Bit of water?" Denko said.

Odin gazed over at Thor and me. Feeling suspicious. "Thor. Open one of the other bottles and let him have a little. Tip a little in."

Thor did as requested, and Denko thanked him.

"That it?" Odin grabbed the duct tape, ready to re-up the gag.

Denko's voice was gruff. "Amazing how you two coddle Nick."

I frowned, confused. Who was Nick?

"*Zeus*," Denko clarified. "Bending over backwards for Nick—Zeus. The shit I've heard over the last few days with that bug is pretty fucking comical. Or I guess you could say sad. That would be another word for it. You think if Nick gets to fuck Isis in enough different ways, with you guys serving her up like the slavish assistants that you are, you really think that'll satisfy him?"

"I don't know if I'd go with slavish assistants," Thor said.

"I would," Denko said. "Think about it."

"Okay, that's enough." Right there Odin started ripping off a new gag.

"Ironic is all. This scene I witnessed right here, just now with the three of you. You had an idea of what you all wanted to do—clearly you wanted to very badly—but you stopped because poor Nick might not be able to handle it. What you don't know is that all this time, he's been talking to Isis here about leaving."

My skin went cold. Odin and Thor turned to me, expecting me to say Denko was lying. "No. I mean, yes, but he's taking it out of context," I said.

"He's been talking to her about having her all to himself," Denko continued. "Nothing out of context about that. Ask her. Tell them, Isis. Tell them about Zeus. The walking-down-the-aisle discussion you two had?"

"He's twisting it all around. It wasn't like a real conversation. He's messing with you."

My men's eyes stayed riveted on me, raw with emotion.

"Were you speaking in code? Was that it?" Denko asked

smugly. "Is *walking down the aisle* a special code for something? Dancing to lame 1990s wedding songs. Is that a metaphor? Did I take all of that too literally?"

The tape strip dangled from Odin's finger. "Is it true?"

"Of course it is," Denko butted in. "The white picket fence? A bit more vanilla than the typical fantasies running through here—"

"You guys, it wasn't like he was trying to get me to leave," I said. "Don't let him make you think that. It was Zeus feeling sad about never having that stuff, that's all."

The hurt in Thor's eyes broke my heart.

Odin stepped toward me. "Did he ask you to marry him?"

My mouth went dry. "What?"

Odin's gaze was dark, and not in a hot way—in an angry way. I'd never seen him like this. "Did he or did he not ask you to marry him? Because in my experience, when a person is talking about a wedding and a home, that's usually in the context of a proposal."

"No," I breathed.

It wasn't a proposal. Was it?

"No!" I continued. "Come on. You know him. It was some-day-never stuff."

"Not what it sounded like to me," Denko said.

"Shut up!" I said. "You don't know. You don't get us."

Odin's voice lowered to a growl. "When a man tells you he wants to dance with you to lame wedding songs..."

Knock-knock. Knock-knock.

Zeus.

I stiffened.

"Yeah," Odin said, speaking in a tone that let him know things were under control.

They were anything but.

The door opened, and there he was.

Chapter Nineteen

ZEUS STROLLED INTO THE ROOM AND SHUT THE DOOR behind him.

"What the hell?" He glowered at Denko, full of heat and testosterone, green eyes looking nearly backlit.

"You just missed it," Denko said. "Rashad and Christian here were trying to get your girlfriend to fuck them in front of me. She almost went for it. It was quite the show."

"Stop it! Don't listen to this guy!" I said.

Zeus just stood there, displaying the kind of calm I'd learned not to trust. "Have you always been a snitch, or is this a skill you've developed as a ZOX agent?"

"He's trying to drive a wedge between us," I said.

"You don't need any help from me," Denko said.

"Can we get that duct tape on?" I wanted him to stop talking and also to stop using their real names.

"Good idea," Thor said.

Zeus grabbed the tape.

"You're done, and you know it," Denko was talking fast now. "You know, Nick, if it wasn't for Isis, they'd be fucking like rabbits right now, and I'd be watching. Is that what you want for your life?"

Zeus shot a dark glance toward Odin and Thor.

"Well, at least we weren't asking her to elope," Odin said. "White picket fence, anyone?"

Zeus's face went white. I could see our conversation gliding through his mind. Odin would've texted him with the details of the bugged purse. "Is that what this motherfucker wants you to believe? You really fucking think that?" He worked at the tape, awash in betrayal.

"Groups like yours always break up—I don't have to tell you that. Criminal organizations. Rock bands. There's a certain shelf life. The question is, who gets the short stick?"

"I don't give a shit about other groups," Odin said defiantly. "Nobody controls us. Nobody predicts us. Nobody tells us what to do." He was saying it to Denko, but it was a message for Zeus, too.

Their fucking power struggle.

Thor came up and slung an arm around my shoulder and looked right at Zeus. Taking Odin's side. Thor didn't like control, either. But I could feel his distress underneath, like a knife in my gut. Could Zeus feel it?

I pulled away from Thor and faced my men. "We're all okay as long as we're together."

"How about if two of us walk down the aisle to dance to lame wedding songs?" Odin said. "Are we okay then?"

"Odin—" I said.

"That's right, Zeus," Odin said. "Denko gave us the whole recap."

"So let me get this straight. It's not okay for me to imagine a thing," Zeus said, "but you three can act on something so fucking out of bounds—"

"You don't get to say what's *fucking-g* in bounds and out of bounds," Odin spat.

"Bringing Denko into things?" Zeus said. "That's out of bounds."

"Says who?"

"Stop it!" Things were deeply, deeply fucked up, and not in a fun way that I liked.

"You think you can start a fucking business?" Denko barked. "Own property? You really think you can have that?"

"That's it." I grabbed the tape from Zeus and tried to free a piece. The end got twisted and stuck together but I pulled a whole bunch off and just pressed it over his mouth. An end flapped loose and got stuck on his shirt.

Zeus angrily snatched the roll and started pulling more off, but not before Denko managed to dislodge the piece I'd put on by shaking around his head. "This is your chance, Nick. Cooperate and I'll give you the white picket fence. The freedom you and Isis want. You can have that."

"Fuck you," Zeus said.

"Things will only go bad from here," Denko said. "You know how these systems work. You know how groups break apart. Your friends wanted to fuck the woman you love in front of your worst enemy. They don't give a crap about your wishes. They were going to do that. They were—"

Crack.

A quick uppercut and Denko was out. Zeus slapped the tape over his mouth all the same.

And then there was this awful silence. The hit had sounded hard.

"I have a lead," Zeus said. "Time-sensitive. All the shit is pointing at Handsome Jack."

Thor went over to our unconscious would-be captor and pulled up the man's eyelids, looking at his pupils.

"Does he look okay?" Zeus asked.

"Nothing Odin's duct tape mummy head won't cure," Thor said.

Zeus smiled wistfully, but the damage was done. The damage felt deep. Scary.

I wrapped my arms around my middle. "We need to talk about this."

Crickets.

"You guys—"

"I don't want to talk about it," Zeus said.

Odin glowered at nothing. Thor stared at the door, arms crossed. The sense of betrayal in the room cut deep.

"You guys, we need to fix this."

More silence. My pulse raced. Did they not feel like it could be fixed?

"We can do anything together," I said.

"I'll be honest with you, Ice, right about now, I just want to finish this thing for Herk." Zeus buttoned his suit jacket and looked at each of us, one at a time. "Let's go. Together. We'll put Denko in the trunk of my ride and fix this for Herk."

My belly twisted because all I could hear was, *let's fix something we can actually fix, and then we're done.*

I said, "I don't like us going into the danger not perfectly together."

Odin was already strapping up, holster to leg, buckle to the shoulder, chamber in, chamber in.

Thor came to me, pocketing his silver Sig. "Need time," he said softly.

I nodded, unconvinced.

"Time," he said. "And maybe if we could find this guy and fuck him up really, really bad together." It was a little bit of a joke, but I could see he was scared, too.

"You guys," I breathed, "what about ZOX knowing where we're going and who we're after? What about that?"

"They'll be focused on Denko now," Odin said. "They'll be looking to get him safe, and they'll be looking for us to escape. It would never cross their minds that we'd stay to solve this mystery."

"Nobody in their right mind would do that," Zeus growled, smashing his chamber into his gun.

"And luckily we're in our right minds," I said. "Right?"

Thor looked grave. "The last place they'd expect us to turn up would be Handsome Jack's."

"Because we are *fucking-g* badass," Odin said. But the spark had gone out of it.

Chapter Twenty

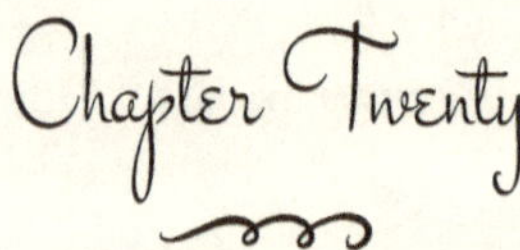

UNDER THE COVER OF DARKNESS, WE PUT A FULLY
trussed-up Denko in the trunk of the old Lincoln that Zeus had
arrived in. Odin rode up front and I rode in back with Thor, just
like old times, but this was nothing like old times. It was new
times. Dark times. I hated that we were risking everything while we
were in a fight. We needed to talk about our relationship! Why
couldn't they see that? Was this like cavemen going out and
hunting together instead of hashing it out?

Zeus briefed us on the way there. He told us that Galvano's
enforcers had both known that the old man was going to hand off
territory. And when pressed, one of the enforcers revealed that he'd
told Nico.

"Nico and Handsome Jack are behind it," Zeus said. "I'm not
sure how it's working, but they're behind it."

"We'll find out," Odin said. "That's why God gave people
vocal cords."

It was four in the morning, but my guys felt sure Handsome
Jack would be in his bar. They thought ZOX might have a skeleton
crew staking out the bar just in case, so they made a plan to case the
area first. All very normal.

Or more like, *air quotes normal.*

I waited at the wheel while my guys melted into the darkness of the neighborhood around Handsome Jack's bar, casing every car and van for ZOX inhabitants, and taking into account every possible window looking out onto the shitty little bar.

Zeus had promised they'd keep me in sight while they inspected the terrain, and I knew they would, but still, I was hyper-aware of Agent Denko in the trunk. It wouldn't go well for me to be arrested with him in the trunk. Then again, what kind of arrest *would* go well?

Fifteen minutes later, Thor came back and joined me in the front, and then Odin squeezed in next to him, and Zeus had to get in the back. I didn't like the configuration—it felt too emblematic of our struggle.

"They don't have anyone here," Odin said. "They thought we'd take off like frightened rabbits."

Zeus grunted. "They really don't know us at all."

Silence.

"This is a beautiful ride," I said, tracing my finger over the classic silver detailing on the steering wheel. Was I doing it too, now? Wanting to talk about anything else but our problems?

Screw that, I thought.

"I love you guys. And I love our family," I said. "And I'll fight for it. What we have is worth fighting for."

"We love you, too." Thor said, but in a tone that said, *don't get mushy.* "Now pull around back. Let's do this thing."

I put the Lincoln into gear and turned into the alley. "Should I wait?"

"No. Safest place for you is with us," Zeus said.

"Always," Odin said. But even that felt wrong. Like an echo of the sort of thing we'd say.

I pulled into a spot next to a dumpster and some stacked-up crates. We got out and clicked the doors closed, quiet as mice.

Handsome Jack's red BMW stood next to the back entrance

under the lone security light. Odin picked the back lock in record time, and we walked in.

An alarm started whining. Odin pulled a small circuit board from his pocket and got to work, ripping the face off the box and winding wires around it. The alarm quieted. Then he simply tore the box off of the wall and threw it across the kitchen.

An unnecessary extra. Not a good sign—Odin was usually economical.

Zeus was already heading into the back with Thor right behind him.

Odin didn't follow just yet. He nudged me into a corner, and then I saw what he saw: a man at the far end of the place with a mop in his hand and earbuds on, just staring at us. Odin made a motion for the man to take his earbuds from his ears. The man complied. Odin crooked his finger and the man came to us.

"You want to live?" Odin whispered.

The man nodded.

He hugged the man to him and whispered into his ear.

The man turned pale and nodded.

"Come on." Odin pushed him back. I followed.

The first person I saw in the back room was Thor, looking hot and pissed off, weapon loose in his hand, but ready for action. He was focused on Handsome Jack, who stood against the wall, ball cap askew, next to Len, the bald-headed, high-end muscle guy.

Zeus was behind the desk at the computer. "PayPal password. Now."

"You can't ask me for that kind of information," Jack said.

Zeus got this scary smile of disbelief just then. Like a kid in the most bafflingly wondrous candy store ever...if the kid was Zeus's fists and the candy store was Handsome Jack's face.

Jack blurted out a string of numbers, a capital letter, a hash tag, and an exclamation mark.

Odin moved around to stand behind Zeus. "Good for you, Jack. That's a *fucking-g* high-security password right there."

The man with the mop sat in a corner on a bright orange crate under one of the horse portraits. He'd shoved in his earbuds and focused with laserlike intensity on the basement floor, creating his own little digital world.

This wasn't the first time I found myself wondering what Odin whispered to people to make them do the things he made them do. Probably best not to know.

Zeus tapped on the keyboard.

I noticed a smashed phone on the floor. Handsome Jack's. Maybe he'd heard the alarm and tried to get a call out.

"Look in payment," Odin said. "Payments for services."

"What the fuck? What are you doing?" Jack asked.

"You know what we're doing," Zeus growled.

"He'd hide it the way he hides the whole thing," Odin said. "It'll be something like design services."

"Look at this." Zeus tapped on the screen. "Is this Nico's email?"

Odin looked over. "What do you say? We have a twenty-thousand-dollar payment for design services to NKO005. That feels Nico to me."

Handsome Jack looked very small under his cap suddenly.

"We'll clear that up when Nico gets here." Thor said. "Jack was kind enough to text Nico to have him come by."

"I swear, it wasn't my idea," Jack said. "Galvano and Herk... please, you guys—"

"You think Galvano and Herk are your main problems here?" Odin asked. "You think the wrath of Galvano and Herk is what you need to fear?"

Handsome Jack looked confused.

Odin and Zeus exchanged glances. Either Handsome Jack was an awesome actor, or he wasn't the one who'd turned us in to ZOX. Was it Nico, then?

"Maybe somebody needs to meet Nico at the door right about now," Thor said. "You guys have this?"

"Yup," Odin said.

Thor headed back up the stairs.

"So Nico needed the money," Zeus said. "Was it gambling or the woman?"

"The woman," Handsome Jack said. "He wanted to buy her a Benz and show he could keep her in style, convince her to leave her man. He placed a few bets and lost everything. Then the rumors started about Herk taking over Galvano's shakedown zone once he married the daughter. People were saying Herk was going to raise the percentage and go really hard. There were rumors about the muscle Herk would send, you know, that he'd send the guys he uses to hold his corners—that they'd come around and fucking squeeze us. Fuck everything up." Handsome Jack swallowed—the man was seriously sweating.

Odin leaned back against the wall behind the desk, weapon loose by his side. "And were a lot of those rumors coming out of Nico's mouth?"

Handsome Jack shot a look at Len. "Not directly...but looking back, he could've been the source, yeah."

"Goddamn," Len said.

"I was sitting at the bar one night," Jack continued, "and I asked Nico if there was any chance he'd be getting back with Maria. I joked that I'd pay him for his stud services if he could win back Maria and break her and Herk up. That's when he thought up the Corvette plan." Handsome Jack looked away, unhappy, distraught. "Or anyway, that's when he *pretended* to think it up. Like the notion of breaking them up or at least getting Don Galvano pissed off at Herk was my idea."

"Fucker played you," Len said. "Probably had it in mind the whole time."

"Getting me scared and offering a solution," Jack said. "Fucker led me into it. He said he'd nix the takeover if I'd erase his debt and give him twenty K besides. It sounded like a good ROI."

"And Nico gets a nice payoff for a joyride," Zeus said.

"And he knew the estate. Knew the garage codes."

"Did you create the fake surveillance of him being here that night beforehand, or once you knew we were coming?"

"Beforehand. Just in case. But Nico said the old man would believe Herk did it in a second. He never imagined Herk would—" He waved his hand at Zeus and Odin.

Hire us.

Odin walked up to him, looked him straight in the eye. "Did you drop the dime on us?"

"Wait, what?" Handsome Jack's eyes nearly popped out of his skull. "What? No. Never. Never—Odin. *Guys—*"

Odin just watched him.

"I swear to you," Handsome Jack said. "Look, I'm willing to cop to my part of it but..." He shook his head fervently. "It was fucked up. I got spooked with what I heard of Herk's plans. But I wouldn't go to the feds. You gotta believe me."

Odin turned. Shook his head. Not Handsome Jack.

Nico, then.

Steps in the hall. Thor ushered Nico back and then shoved him into Zeus's waiting arms. Zeus pulled him upright and cracked him in the jaw and Nico was down.

"Get the fuck up," Odin growled.

Nico stayed on the floor, lip bleeding, hands up in a defensive posture. Here he was, this man who had nearly gotten us killed. Still might. Why should I feel sorry for him? But I did.

"Don't kill him," I said. "Don't kill him."

"Give me one good reason," Odin said.

"Because he can't confess to Galvano?"

Zeus growled. Thor snorted. Both acting so unconvinced.

Oh, I got it. I was the good cop here.

"I'll tell him," Nico said. "I'll tell everything."

"You have the wig?" Thor asked.

"I tossed it in the ravine a mile from the car," Nico said. "But I'll tell him where it is if he wants to check."

"And you'll tell the whole fucking story with every other detail he'd care to validate?" Thor asked.

Nico nodded and proclaimed yes and swore in every way he could.

It was stupid, but I really did feel sorry for Nico, cowering on the floor of Handsome Jack's back room. Nico had done it for love, and now not only would he likely lose the woman he loved due to not having the money he'd probably pretended to have, but he was also about to be in deep shit with Galvano and Herk. And yeah, we were forced back on the run, but at least we had each other.

Or did we?

My guys presented a fiercely united front, but maybe that's all we had—a united front and a dangerous federal agent tied up in the trunk of our stolen car.

I got this hollow feeling in my belly as Zeus called Herk and then Galvano. Galvano suggested we meet behind an abandoned warehouse on Alameda Street.

"Please," Handsome Jack begged. "Aren't I just another victim in this?"

"Yeah, you're a victim of your willingness to believe the worst of a brown guy," Odin snarled.

We headed out back. Zeus threw Nico in the trunk with Agent Denko.

"Gotta love the trunk on a Lincoln," Thor said. Handsome Jack rode in the back between Thor and me, using the time to beg us to let him go, beg us to make the case to Don Galvano that he'd been hoodwinked by Nico.

Around midway there he was offering us money. That bought him a strip of duct tape over his mouth.

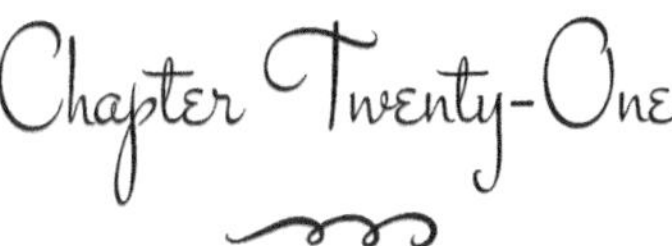

Chapter Twenty-One

GALVANO'S WAREHOUSE WAS A FREESTANDING concrete building with the words *cold storage* splashed above boarded-up windows and a door crisscrossed with bars. We drove around back and pulled in between two other cars—Don Galvano's and Herk's.

They both got out when we arrived. Thor unlocked the door while Odin pulled Handsome Jack from the back seat. Zeus opened the trunk and pulled Nico out.

Galvano furrowed his brow when he spotted Denko still in there. "Three? I thought you said two."

"That one's for us," Zeus said, slamming the trunk.

Galvano nodded. Because apparently bad guys don't need more explanation for that sort of thing. *For us.* Like, what are we? Vampires?

Herk greeted us, but things were definitely cold between him and Don Galvano. And two big dangerous guys like that generated a lot of cold.

We went inside. Zeus put them both on the floor, and then he jabbed Nico with his foot. "You don't want to make me tell it."

Nico told the story. He'd wanted a car for Sophia Viga and

some nicer furnishings. He hadn't meant to hurt anyone. He went on and on, apologizing profusely for crashing the Corvette.

"Nico put the scare into Handsome Jack," Odin said. And it was a sort of kindness to Handsome Jack that he'd say that.

Galvano looked furious. "You two try to play me? And you fuck things up between my daughter and the man she loves? You think you can do that?" He gave Herk a look. "Herk. My apologies."

Herk nodded.

Galvano turned again to Nico. "You fuck with my family?"

My heart pounded. Galvano had called Herk family. It was sweet in a kind of Hallmark moment way...if you ignored what would happen once we left.

Galvano went and clasped Herk's hand and arm at the same time. "You said you didn't crash my 'vette and I didn't take your word. I am beyond sorry. I see this here now, what really happened..."

"It's okay," Herk said.

"No, it's not okay. You're a man of your word, and I know how deeply fucking grievous it is to not be taken at that when you're a man of your word."

"I'm glad we cleared it up," Herk said. "It means a lot, being right with you. For Maria."

"It means a fucking lot that you pursued this. We'll rethink this Oxford thing. I was mistaken there. I'll be proud to have you in our family. Not just proud. Lucky you fucking saw it through. And you guys." He let Herk go and turned to us. "I'm grateful as hell you worked this shit out. Masterful."

Herk took Zeus's hand, going on to shake with all of us, even me, saying a heartfelt *thank you* to each and every one of us.

"We have this," Galvano continued, turning to my guys. "And all payment is on me. Whatever your fee, you'll send me the bill."

Together they looked down at Handsome Jack and Nico.

Father and prospective son-in-law together. It reminded me of how, back in the farming community where I grew up, prospective sons-in-law would frequently help their fiancée's family with things like barn repairs or harvesting crops. Plying their trade together.

"Stupid motherfucker," Herk said to Handsome Jack. "I would've fucking lowered your rate. I wouldn't have used muscle—not for first-round collections. I always automate any kind of first-round collections. It saves money on enforcement muscle. Enforcement muscle is fucking expensive."

Don Galvano turned to Herk with a look of respect.

"Don't kill them," I said suddenly.

All eyes were on me.

"Ice," Zeus said. "You can't ask that."

"It's what I want." I wanted our gang back together. And for nobody to die. I wanted the moon. I wanted the world safe for love.

"We'll see," Galvano said.

Odin grabbed my hand and pulled me out to the car. He and Zeus got up front as usual. Thor checked on Denko and then got in the back with me. Our usual driving formation.

"Will they kill them?" I asked.

"No," Zeus said. "Shit, Ice, asking a thing like that?"

"I had to," I bit out.

Thor gave me an appreciative look. "That's why you rock."

We headed out onto the dark street in solemn silence. Maybe Nico and Handsome Jack would be spared, but we might not be so lucky, riding along with a dangerous agent in the car trunk and two elephants in the car—Zeus, threatened by us almost fucking in front of Denko, and Thor and Odin threatened by Zeus's picket-fence dream.

"So fucking Millennial of Herk, what with the automation," Thor said.

"No doubt," I said, grateful for any conversation at this point.

"Somehow I don't think Handsome Jack's rate is going to get lowered now."

"One big happy family," Thor said.

"I can just see their Christmas dinners now," I tried. "*Herk, you're saving money on enforcement muscle? Wow that's brilliant— it really such an annoying expense to have a guy threatened every other fucking day. Yeah, that's right, Poppa, and if you lower rates, you have to break less kneecaps, which pays for itself. Could you please pass the Baby Jesus cradle gravy boat? Why, thank you.*"

No go.

"What do you think traffic's like on the fifteen right now?" Zeus asked.

"Does it matter?" Thor stretched out and slung an arm around me. "I see blackjack in our future."

"Wait, Vegas?" I asked. "What about Honolulu?"

"We need to get out of L.A.," Thor said.

I sat back. "Are we going to send Galvano a bill?"

"No way," Zeus said. "We'll send him a card. Best to make solving this case a gift from us. A nice wedding gift."

"Isn't a couple's enemies bound with duct tape and bleeding at their feet more of a tenth-anniversary gift?" I said. "Oh, wait. That's lace."

They didn't even laugh.

I was starting to feel panicky, like our beautiful family was slipping away.

"If we let Agent Denko fuck us up, he wins," I said.

"Not exactly," Odin said. "In that scenario nobody wins."

Okay.

Dawn was breaking. We zoomed around one turnpike and then another, and shot off west. The tires hummed, adding to the buzz of tension in the car. We'd never been so far apart from each other before—far apart and drifting further with alarming speed.

Having Agent Denko in the trunk was not helping things. My guys were in vigilance overdrive, all hyperfocused on the mirrors, on the road. Taking in every detail, knowing every agent in the Southwest would be hunting for him by now.

Twice Zeus pulled off the highway to change things up. We'd swing through strip malls, past fast food and quick-stop franchises, all of those colorful logos promising consistency and familiarity. Just then I could see the appeal.

"Remember when ZOX found you that first night?" I asked. "When I was first with you, and Zeus was down in the weight room. We three were upstairs in the suite, and that guy came in like a room service waiter? Remember? And we got out on the roof?"

"Mmm," Odin said. "And the agent took you hostage down there, and Zeus threatened to shoot him through your head."

Not exactly the point I was going for. "That's the first time I understood what family meant for you. All the agents were crawling all over, all out to kill you, and you guys wouldn't leave without Zeus. That was when I first loved you—all of you."

Thor looked at me sadly. He knew what I was trying to do.

"You were willing to die for each other," I continued. "I'd never felt anything like that before. I'd been so into thrills and bungee jumping and all of that sort of shit, but here was something so beyond. Willing to die for love. For your fucking brothers."

Silence. *Give it up,* that's what the silence said.

Fuck it. I'd never give up on us—not ever.

"That's the real danger—love," I said. "Love is dangerous. That's what makes it worth something. Love is the ultimate cliff to jump over, and I'll do it again and again, knowing you guys are there. I'll blow everything, give everything, because that's what we do for each other. You taught me how to love like that."

I imagined, during the long silence that followed, that I'd gotten through to them. I even felt a little bit hopeful.

"You *taught* me it," I said again.

"Love isn't enough," Odin said finally. "You need trust, Ice. This is the problem that we have."

"We *have* trust."

"No," he said sadly. "Zeus and you talked about marriage, about making a life together—the two of you without us."

"And you nearly brought another person into the mix," Zeus growled. "It's a kind of cheating. I don't fucking care—it's cheating."

"It wasn't cheating," Thor said. "It was being what we are. It was us expressing our love."

"With Denko in the mix?" Zeus asked.

"He wasn't in the mix," Thor said. "We do fucked-up things all the time—that's us."

"We do fucked-up things *inside our group*," Zeus said. "We love and accept each other inside ourselves. Just because some married couple out there decides they like to buttfuck, it doesn't mean they suddenly get to buttfuck other people."

"This was in no way like fucking Denko," Thor said.

Zeus snorted. "Are you kidding me? Whether he's shoving his cock into Isis, holding a dildo, or watching, that's involving him. What we do is an expression of our love. Bringing him into our mix is involving him."

"No, our total freedom to be fucked up and dirty is an expression of our love," Thor said, "and a few weeks ago you would've been on board with that. You're moving the line, Zeus, and you don't get to do that."

"Fucking is romantic, and we are a romantic unit of four," Zeus bit out. "Where Denko doesn't belong."

"A romantic unit of four? Are we?" Odin barked. "That's funny, because explain to me how two can plan to secretly break off and get married."

"Nobody was planning that," I said. "There were no plans. You have to be free to talk about dreams—"

"Dreams?" Thor said. "Dreams are the first step of everything. Haven't you ever heard that saying, *in dreams begin reality?*"

"That's not how it was," I said.

"No?" Odin said. "Zeus, you're familiar with the concept, are you not? You first start them thinking about it. Visualization."

"Fuck you," Zeus said. "Yeah, I wanted to visualize that. Yes, I wanted the woman I love to visualize that with me. You want to pretend you've never visualized something other than this? Are you the fucking dream police now?"

"Are you the arbiter of what is appropriately fucked up and what is wrongly fucked up?" Odin snapped.

"Stop it, you guys!"

Odin ignored my pleas. "I don't want to go through my days wondering if I'm crossing some ever-moving line for you. Anything consensual, that's what we're doing here. We can be as fucked up as we want as long as it's consensual—"

"Unless it's cheating!" Zeus angrily changed lanes. He was speeding. Everything was spinning out of control. I couldn't believe the car itself wasn't spinning.

"It didn't feel like cheating," I said, trying to calm things. "It felt like it was about us and what we wanted. And talking about a wedding didn't feel like planning. It was just about love. God, you guys!"

Zeus turned on the music. Some stupid '90s pop stuff. Odin stared out the window, utterly dug in.

I pressed my face into Thor's warm, solid shoulder. We'd done a beautiful thing together. We'd saved that family. Couldn't we save ours?

And since when was Zeus so rigid about what we could and couldn't do? It was true—he'd moved that line, and that wasn't like him.

And another thing: in the past, Odin had always been patient with Zeus, balancing him, working with him. Now he had no tolerance.

What wasn't I seeing?

I closed my eyes, thinking about those first days we were together. The rush of excitement the week before my first robbery with them. It seemed forever ago, us drunk and wearing wigs and dancing on the tabletop of our hotel suite to Michael Jackson.

My bank robbers had been betrayed in the worst way by their own country, and they didn't let it make them small—they'd grown big and bold. They'd found love and brotherhood in the wreckage. Like the losers who get kicked out of a fabulous night-club, but instead of going meekly, they go up and do the most amazing dance on the club stage where nobody can touch them.

Thor did a little rubbing thing on my shoulder that mixed with the lulling sound of the engine. The sun was up now, but none of us had slept. I found that I was so sleepy. So very sleepy.

Chapter Twenty-Two

I WOKE UP—OR MORE ACCURATELY, GOT *WOKEN* UP—BY Thor shaking me.

"Where are we?" I asked, rubbing my eyes.

"Vegas, baby," Thor said.

I sat up. "What time is it?"

"After lunch, sleepyhead." He pulled me out from the car. He was wearing a nice suit. I rubbed my eyes and peered around. We were in the dark corner of some sort of parking ramp full of cars—rows and rows of shiny cars like bullets in the dark. Out beyond the concrete slats of the ramp, it was daylight. More like daylight plus, with flashing lights and jagged energy in the air.

Odin strolled over in a suit and tie, attention all around, hyper-aware. He didn't like being in an area with so many hiding places.

Right behind Odin was Zeus wheeling a dolly with a giant, brightly painted magician's trick box strapped onto it—the kind where you shut somebody in and pretend you're cutting them in half. It was here I realized Thor was actually in tails, like a magician.

"What the fuck?" I said.

"We have to get him inside a room," Odin said. "He won't be out cold forever."

"Motherfucker, no way," I said. "He's in there?"

"We can't leave him in the trunk." Odin shrugged. "Nothing like hiding in plain sight."

"Where'd you even get that?"

"Rented," Zeus said. "While you snored away."

I smiled, knowing they'd probably moved around stealthily, as only they could, using all of their mad covert ops skills to ensure I stayed sleeping. Maybe it gave them something to discuss and focus on. Something to work together on. But nothing was different—that deep sense of sorrow and betrayal permeated the air between us.

Women all over the world complain that their men don't want to talk about their relationship. They think they have it bad? They should try tripling the number of men in their romantic unit and see how relationship talks go then.

Zeus handed me a clear garment bag with something sparkly inside—a sexy magician's assistant outfit. "Just carry it," he said.

I tried to think of a joke to make to lighten the mood, like, magician role-play was a kink I couldn't go for, or, if they started with the magic tricks I might have to safeword out.

I didn't have it in me. So I just I grabbed the bag. "Thanks."

"You and Thor," Zeus said, "you're here for tryouts down at the Ritz. It's booked, but they're using this as an overflow hotel. Odin and I are helpful friends." He handed me new ID.

"Wow." I took it and examined it, memorizing my new name. "You got ahold of a go bag while I was sleeping, too? Fuck, did you also cure cancer?"

Odin grinned and messed up my hair.

I smoothed it down. "So...what? We're just here?"

"Until we leave," Zeus said, handing me a dark curly wig. "We survive."

Survival. Was that all that was left of our beautiful love? Survival? "We need to talk about this," I said.

"Women," Zeus growled.

None of them took the bait. At least they had something to agree on. I used the reflection of the windows to fix my wig. We'd wait out the danger and then what? Go our separate ways? Splitting up would be safer, but that had always been the case, and it was never what we did. We stayed together. We were all about the fuck you. *You WISH we were dead, motherfuckers,* like our tattoos said.

I put on a coat of red lipstick. And sure, I'd enjoyed hearing Zeus's dream, but it was just a fairy tale. I'd never want to leave my guys, and I knew Zeus wouldn't want that either—couldn't they see that? And we'd never betray Zeus in our hearts by bringing in a fourth guy in any meaningful way.

Why were they being so stubborn?

I tucked in some stray blonde hairs. Odin nodded. He always did like me as a brunette.

We headed down to ground level to the street, which was awash with lights and crazy grandeur. I'd never seen anything like it. "It's like..." I was going to say a carnival funhouse nightmare, but that wasn't it. "It's like...."

"Poor little sheep farmer," Odin said. "I always forget that's what you were."

"What it's *like* is Vegas," Zeus said. "Only Vegas is like Vegas."

Thor took my hand and pulled me across the busy, noisy traffic jam. We made our way down the sidewalk packed with people in all kinds of clothes, from red carpet stuff to *Les Miserables* beggar-wear to your classic "I'm a freak on stilts" look.

Every hotel casino had a theme—there was a Roman deca-dence place, a cowboy place, a circus place. Thor kept hold of my hand, which was good, because I couldn't stop gaping at it all. At one point, I thought Zeus might haul off and hit one of the guys handing out fliers.

We finally found our hotel, which had a fancy Italian theme, all marble and Michelangelo, though the soundtrack was *dings* and *doot-doot-doots* and *cha-chings* coming from the slot machines, a weirdly agitating noise that didn't do much to calm me.

Thor and I checked in. He told the clerk we were from Nebraska and waved a hand at Zeus and Odin, suggesting they were our assistants, not really with us, nothing to see. Zeus and Odin stood obediently by, having changed their demeanors to make themselves seem small and unremarkable, a truly amazing feat, considering. She wished us luck on the act and gave us our key cards.

Zeus and Odin rolled the box into the ginormous elevator. Thor hit the button for our floor. We didn't talk all the way up to the twenty-seventh floor and down the hall to our suite.

The place was way more over the top than our usual spots, with everything overstuffed and megafancy and ultraposh, all marble and gold and silk with a hot tub fit for a prince, but fake somehow. It was all very full, yet all very empty.

They set the magician's box in the corner, like it was just some stupid piece of luggage.

"Why do we have to keep him?" I asked. "You think they're close?"

Thor shrugged. "You always want insurance." An understatement. They would've ditched him if they had felt safe.

They set about exploring the room, stashing weapons, looking at potential escape routes. I waited in the lounge area at the center of the overly decorated suite.

"What the fuck," I said when Zeus strolled back in.

"Welcome to Vegas," he said, knowing exactly what the fuck my *what the fuck* was about.

When the inspection was complete, they opened up the box, and there was Denko slumped in the bottom, gagged, wrists and ankles bound in duct tape. Thor knelt in front of him and checked his pulse, then he pulled up his eyelids. "He's good." He pulled the tape off his mouth and slapped his cheeks. "Hey."

The man mumbled. He and Odin carried him across the suite and propped him up on some cushions in the corner by the window, which had what I suppose was technically a great view of the Eiffel Tower except it wasn't the Eiffel Tower.

"Did you put him by the window so we can watch him while we look at the view?" I asked.

"Of course," Zeus said.

Professionals to the end.

"And you're sure he's okay?"

"Don't be fooled," Thor said. "He's as alert and energetic as we are."

Odin strolled off to a corner bar dripping with mirrored crystal. He grabbed what was no doubt a zillion-dollar bottle of scotch, twisted off the cap, and poured himself a drink. Thor went over and pulled a bottle of water from the small refrigerator. He brought it over to Denko, crouching, tipping the bottle into his mouth, taking care not to spill it all over him.

Denko drank pretty competently for a tied-up man. So maybe he was alert.

Zeus got on the phone and ordered a snack and sandwich cart to be left out in the hall. "Knock when it's out there and we'll grab it," he said. Prudent, what with Denko like that. There were limits to hiding in plain sight, even here.

I strolled around the place. Two bedrooms with the usual spa-like bathroom. I returned to the main room and sunk into the couch. I didn't like it. We were fake getting along, and now we were in this fake place. "I wish we hadn't come here," I said.

Thor sunk down on one side of me; Zeus sat on my other side. Odin came over with a scotch and handed it down to Zeus.

A peace offering?

Zeus threw it back in a gulp.

"Just a matter of time," Denko said from across the room. "We're on your ass. You have to know it."

Odin grinned at Denko. Odin usually had a beautiful smile, all dark tousled hair and gorgeous lashes and that glint in his golden eyes, but this smile wasn't beautiful; it was a cold, harsh *fuck you* smile.

"Every fucking resource, pointing at you," Denko said. "You think this hotel didn't get a bulletin? You've been out of the agency all these years; you have no idea what we can do now. How close we can track."

"Hasn't done you much good so far," Zeus said in his fake calm voice.

His fake calm voice.

Fuck.

How much trouble were we in?

"And when my men come for you—we're talking minutes more than hours—this sea of civilians will not keep you safe."

Thor crossed his legs. "Using civilians to keep safe isn't our style anyway."

"Have you thought about what I said, Nick?" Denko asked suddenly. "You could make her happy."

"You want duct tape over your mouth for when the snacks come?" Zeus grumbled. "Is that what you want?"

"You could have a home, Nick. Children. A place in the community."

Odin headed back for the bar. "Who's gonna dig out the duct tape? I hope we packed it on top."

"Yeah," I said. "Denko doesn't have any problems some duct tape can't fix."

Thor smiled at this.

Here was something we could agree on. *Unite against Agent Denko!* I thought. *He's a common enemy!*

"Let him say what he wants," Zeus grumbled. "It doesn't matter."

Denko addressed Odin. "You know how Nick came to choose La Belle, Rashad? How he heard it was the best?"

"Don't know, don't care." Odin poured himself another glass of scotch.

I frowned, hating that this guy knew things that we didn't know about each other. Did it really not bother Odin?

"Tell them what day Valentine's Day is, Nick. Tell them the significance of it."

Zeus glared. "You think you know important things, but you don't know shit."

Thor stared at his own fingernails, but I could tell he was curious.

Zeus heaved himself up off the couch and joined Odin at the bar. Odin topped off his scotch. "Goddess? Want a drink?"

"Nothing," I said.

"Fine, I'll tell them," Denko continued. "Valentine's Day was Nick's parents' anniversary. It's an important day to him in a deep way."

"Nice to see the agency shrink's been so ethical about patient-client confidentiality," Zeus said.

"And where do you think they would celebrate?"

"Here comes Denko with the big reveal," Zeus said. "Or should we wait for the studio audience to guess?"

Shivers went over me. "At La Belle?" I tried. "Zeus, why didn't you say?"

Zeus shrugged.

I wanted more than a shrug. I wanted him to take it seriously. I needed us to be serious. "Zeus, that was your parents' special anniversary place?"

"When they could manage it." Zeus took his scotch with him to the window.

"Tell us," I said.

"It doesn't matter."

"It does to me," I said.

He gazed out with a faraway look. "It was important to them," he said softly. We all waited. He went on, "They really couldn't afford it—it was their splurge. And I'd ask them, why splurge on an anniversary meal at a fancy restaurant when, you know, when we didn't have enough money to get the car fixed and Mom had to bus it to work and Dad had been doing without his medication, and they'd say, *this is where you go when you're happy and in love.*"

It was so sweet. He'd wanted us to carry on the tradition. *Happy and in love.*

"Zeus," I whispered.

He shrugged it off. "So that's how I knew about La Belle. No big. And now we have the money." He came and sat back down with us, avoiding our gazes.

"You had good parents," Denko said. "You were a good boy with good, hard-working parents—the kind of family people dream of having. You three, that fierce closeness."

Zeus glared into the distance. I was thankful Denko didn't know my name, didn't know about how desperately I missed my sisters so that he could taunt me with memories like this.

Denko went on, relentlessly filling in the details of a lost, happy life. Christmas. Little League. Bingo the dog with one black foot. The clockmaker father. Family game night.

Zeus would never have that. He'd always have to keep running. We'd all have to keep running. I stared at my shoes, thinking about what an awesome father Zeus could've made. He'd be the kind to coach a soccer team. Fix things.

Denko went on. Zeus's father had a clock shop in the neighborhood that he could walk to. Zeus would hang out there after school with Bingo.

Nobody stopped Denko. Should somebody stop him?

But then I realized that it was up to Zeus to stop him.

Why wasn't Zeus stopping him?

That's when I got it—Zeus loved the respite of his past. He loved it the way when, after you've been driving for hours and you're tired, you rest your eyes—and you love that quick rest. A dangerous, seductive kind of rest. He missed the regular world. A regular life. Is that why he'd wanted us at La Belle? To pretend for a while?

He looked so alone. I put my arm around him, but still he seemed alone.

"And the way you and your mother cared for your dad at the end—that togetherness you had," Denko continued. "We pulled you off that case in Yemen and sent you back—we knew you would've gone AWOL if we hadn't. Your little family against that devastating disease. Remember how you fought for him? And your mother...you lost them too soon."

Zeus looked bereft. I glanced at Thor, whose ordinarily sunny, happy eyes had lost some brightness. Odin furrowed his brows.

"You probably thought you could never have it again, but you see that you can with Isis. You see it. Even I see it," Denko continued. "Isis has a good heart like that. You and her. It's within your grasp."

"We all have good hearts like that," Zeus spat.

"That house is for sale," Denko said.

Zeus stiffened. "What?"

"You know—561 Oak Mill Terrace. It's been on the market for a while. It needs a little repair, of course. Remember how you and your father brought one of your mother's yellow roses to the paint store to match it? The house it still that color. South side needs a new coat, though. Overhang is still leaking. The roses could use some TLC."

My heart pounded. Even I had this urge to rescue the house. Fix it.

"Liar."

"You think I would lie about something so easy to check? Go see for yourself."

Odin's voice sounded distant. "Zeus."

Zeus shrugged. "Don't worry."

"Don't worry?" Odin barked. "You think I don't know how much you loved them?"

Zeus shrugged.

"How much you miss them?" Odin said.

Another shrug.

"Don't shrug me off." Odin pushed away from the bar and moved near. "Why didn't you say what La Belle meant?"

"I don't know," Zeus said.

"Let's do some business, Nick," Denko said. "It would be so easy—"

Zeus shot Denko a look so hard, so full of fury, it would stop a tornado in its tracks. I pulled my arm away. Denko stopped talking. It chilled the whole room—even the poshness frenzy seemed to calm.

I laid a hand on his arm. "Zeus."

"It's not just about the anniversary." He looked at all of us—me, Thor, Odin. "I'm going to be honest, I've been freaking out." He stood and took a few steps around, unsure, it seemed, where to go, what to do with himself. He gazed out at fake Paris.

None of us dared to speak.

"Since I was a kid, one of my greatest dreams has been to have a family just the one I grew up in. When ZOX recruited me, I never saw it as a career. I wanted to walk down to the same shop every day for thirty years. I wanted that stability and simplicity. Traditions. A simple, normal family. All throughout being in the agency, even through us knocking over banks, I still had that in my mind— that someday I would have that life for my own." He lowered his voice to a whisper. "My family *was* amazing, you guys. You wouldn't believe. Growing up, all I wanted was to be like that— have this stupid, simple life. And yeah, that door's been closed a long time. And I've been realizing that lately, and it's been fucking me up."

So that was the P.I. agency impulse. A shop we could walk to. A way to feel normal.

"And then Herk walked in with all of his talk about how important his family was to him, to hear him describe that life he dreamed of with Maria. Fucking Herk..." Zeus took a ragged breath.

"That door is open," Denko said. "You just have to choose to walk through it."

***

READY FOR MORE BANK ROBBERS? BECAUSE THEY'RE READY FOR YOU!

Three hot bank robbers all to herself: *check*
A fabulous Italian holiday: *check*
Enemies long gone: *check*
Amazing food, clothes, and sex: *check, check, and f&*king check!*

The gang is in full vacation mode, and Isis has never been happier. But then tragedy strikes the farm she had to leave behind—people are dying.

Her sister might be sent to prison for something she didn't do. The farm is in trouble.

Isis is desperate to help, but how can she? It's too dangerous for her sisters to find out she's still alive, too dangerous for the gang to return to the scene of that crime. At least that's what Thor and Zeus think. But Odin's nightmares are back. And he has other ideas...and those ideas might be more dangerous than anything.

The Hard Way - Taken Hostage by Kinky Bank Robbers Book 5

Get fun stuff, freebies, exclusive content, the latest news and more!
The Annika Martin newsletter is the place to be! http://www.an-
nikamartinbooks.com/newletter/

I love hearing from you! Email me at annika@
annikamartinbooks.com
Website: http://annikamartinbooks.com

Let's have some fun!
My friend, if you've gotten this far in the kinky bank robbers,
you definitely belong here>>> https://www.facebook.com/
groups/AnnikaMartinFabulousGang/

Chapter Twenty-Three

I CRINGED AS ZEUS STROLLED OVER TO DENKO. WOULD he put a foot through his face? Knock him out again? Throw him out the window? But he simply stopped. Stood over him. Towered over him.

Zeus seemed larger just then—badass and beautiful. Achingly vulnerable.

Odin went up behind Zeus. "We can never give you that." His voice was full of emotion. "The same house for 30 years. The office down the corner."

"I can give you that," Denko said.

My throat felt thick.

Zeus stared down at Denko. "I love these people. I'd die for these people. I'm grieving a loss, that's all. The loss of that dream. I never quite let go of that boyhood dream, that's all. And when I realized that I could never have all that..." He turned to us then, green eyes burning. "I was scared." He eyed each of us, connecting with each of us. "Scared of doors closing, scared of losing you guys, too. It made me want to clamp down and control you guys harder. And that whole watching thing? I wasn't being honest, either. It wasn't out of line, not for us—who gives a fuck about somebody watching? Even Denko. Making that rule, it was about controlling you and pulling you closer, because I was insecure. But instead of pulling you closer to me, it pushed you away."

Odin put his hand on Zeus's shoulder. "Why didn't you say?"

"That I mourn something impossible that I can never have? That I dream of walking down the aisle someday? It's stupid. And I don't even want it, really—not if it means not having us."

"Don't fool yourself, Nick—it's only going to get worse," Denko said. "The personality mix I'm seeing here is clearly not viable long term. These three live to break rules. Especially Rashad—there is no rule he won't break, no boundary he won't push. He can't help it—it's his patterning, and it will only get worse."

Odin glared at Denko. "*Fucking-g* patterning—fuck you."

"Say what you will, Rashad. You could barely control yourself once you saw Nick making rules."

Odin sniffed.

"You were a bull seeing red. You couldn't think straight. Ice knew he was in pain, but you, his oldest friend, did you have any clue of this? No."

Odin was doing his best to look annoyed, but I could see the horror in his eyes.

"You were a bull charging at a red flag." Denko had a point—Odin had been kind of knee-jerky about the whole thing. "You can't help it. It's how you survived prison."

Odin's stare turned murderous.

"It's how you kept from breaking," Denko continued. "That's what's in you."

I held my breath. Did Denko have a death wish or what?

"Fuck!" Odin sounded surprised. "Fuck!" He turned to Zeus. "I was making you into Mahfoud Ben-sakria. You made a rule, and I reacted like an angry puppet."

Zeus shook his head. "It's not on you—"

"An angry puppet of Mahfoud," Odin said. "The sadist Mahfoud."

I felt Thor straighten beside me. "The prison," he whispered. "That was the warden at the prison where Odin was held."

"I see a rule, and I defy it," Odin continued. "I projected Mahfoud on you. I am sorry for acting like an angry puppet."

"It's okay," Zeus said.

"The prison will never be over for you, Rashad," Denko said. "You'll always be a prisoner."

Odin stormed over, and I thought maybe *he* might kill Denko, but Zeus stopped him, held him by his arms. "I'm sorry. I wasn't thinking of you with the prison."

"You shouldn't have to think of me in the prison," Odin said. "Reacting like a puppet of the sadist Mahfoud instead of seeing my brother in pain? Never again."

"Odin—"

"Right," Odin said. "I can't promise I won't feel that in me. But I can promise to stay vigilant."

"You were right to push back. I was being extreme."

"No, I was being extreme," Odin said. "I was the one."

"No, *I* was being extreme." Playfully, Zeus grabbed Odin's collar. "Do we have to fight now?"

Odin wasn't in a playful mood. "I don't want you to lose your dream."

"You can't fight that battle for me," Zeus said. "Losing that dream? That's my shit to deal with."

"If it's your dream, it's our dream," Odin said.

Zeus still held Odin's collar, but it was different now. Everything had shifted.

"We're here. Let us be your home," Odin said.

Zeus's eyes shone with emotion. I thought he might cry, or maybe kiss him.

"You're never alone," Thor said.

Zeus let Odin go and came over to us. "I'm sorry," he said.

"We're with you," Thor said. "I didn't see what you were struggling with either, but I'll try harder."

Zeus sank into the couch between us. "You have a rebel streak, too. What do you think, Denko?" he called.

Denko said nothing. His plan to show us why we couldn't be together had backfired. He'd shown my guys something important about how to be together.

Odin strolled over.

"Fuck." Zeus looked up at him with utter affection and understanding. Like they'd come through a fire together.

"I know," Odin replied.

I smiled. That was a make-up kiss if I ever saw one. My bank robbers' version, anyway. "I believe in us so much right now," I said.

Nobody replied. We all felt it. We were so beyond words.

Zeus sat back, looking calm. "And really, a tied-up guy watching? Who cares. What the fuck difference does it make? Who am I that I get to say we can't do that? Who am I to deprive Ice of that? Not that I would've thought it up, but it's so hot when Isis gets turned on by super-fucked-up things."

"Hey!" I said, pushing Zeus playfully.

He pulled me up onto his lap. "We're fucking outlaws. We think it, and we do it."

Odin came over behind the couch and set a hand on Zeus's shoulder. "I wasn't carrying you."

Zeus put a hand on Odin's hand. "You always carry me."

"That door doesn't have to be closed," Denko said. "You can still decide—"

"Have you heard nothing?" Zeus said. "We're the God Pack. A family. We love each other. We'll die for each other."

"Though if this ZOX agent gig doesn't work out," Odin said, "you could always look into being a group therapist."

"Yeah." Zeus surged up and slammed his foot onto the coffee table. I was shocked that the thing didn't break apart. Was he going to stand on it?

But then he did something that gave me shivers.

He rolled up his pant leg.

There it was. Our tattoo. The storm cloud with four lightning bolts. He pulled off his shirt and turned his arm to reveal the angel with the scrolls. "You see this tattoo? This says, I choose these people. I unchoose everything else, and that's fine, because these people are my fucking life."

Thor beamed at Zeus. "Though technically it says *You WISH we were dead, motherfuckers.*"

"Yes, technically it says that."

"Because it's *fucking-g awesome.*" Odin was there next to him now, pulling off his shirt, baring his tattoos. "We choose each other. Always."

Thor and I stood up then. Thor rolled up his pant leg and his sleeve. I pulled off my shoe and shoved down my thigh-high stocking and pushed up my sleeve too.

There they were, our tattoos. I could never get enough of looking at them, admiring them, this link we had. My guys couldn't, either. This little display wasn't so much for Denko as it was for us. Denko was small across the room, and we were huge with love, reveling in our family.

"Enjoy it while you can," Denko said.

"I'm so tired of your negativity," I said, pulling my stocking back up. "You're a negative person."

Thor laughed, and I just smiled. Was it possible to be even more in love with my guys?

Zeus flopped back onto the couch and pulled me onto his lap. Thor and Odin flopped down on either side.

I punched Zeus in the arm. "I get turned on by super-fucked-up things? Did I hear you right?"

Zeus wrapped his huge hand around my upper arm, huge and sinewy and strong over my silky blouse. With his other hand, he adjusted the collar of my blouse. "Are you saying it's not fucked-up to want a stern, tied-up man to watch as we slowly unbutton your shirt, goddess?"

He fingered a button. My attention flew to Denko. His eyes a forbidden jagged edge on my skin.

My belly tightened.

Zeus smiled, continuing to finger that button.

Would he?

Odin stood up in front of the couch where Zeus sat with me on his lap. He reached down and smoothed back my hair. "Unbutton her shirt, Zeus."

Shivers exploded across my skin. "You guys," I whispered.

Zeus's eyes were full of love as he began to unbutton my shirt, holding me with his gaze. "What, goddess?"

"Oh my god," I said as his fingers lightly brushed my chest.

"Take your time on every button, Zeus," Odin said. "Let her know that you control everything." He pulled my arms up above my head and hooked my hands around his neck. "Keep your arms just like this, Ice," he growled.

Of course there was nothing I wanted more. I tipped my head up; Odin's hard gaze speared dark excitement clear through me. He squeezed my wrists, holding me in place, reminding me of the dangerous edge of him. "Let her know that her body is ours to use for our utter and complete pleasure," he said.

Yaassss, I thought, letting my eyes drift closed.

I bit back a grin as Zeus flicked open another button. Air cooled my newly bared skin. He was baring me to the air, baring me to Denko's dark eyes.

Odin slid his hands up and down my arms, like he couldn't believe how silky my skin was. "We'll let another man watch if we choose, but we will never allow another to touch you, baby. You are ours to touch—only ours. And we are only yours."

I kissed his belly.

"Well, if it's going to be this kind of party..." Thor got up and headed to where we'd deposited our luggage. Not a minute later, Michael Jackson was on, and not ironically, either. Because my guys were badass like that. *Gotta be Startin' Something* sounded out. He stalked back over and sat on the couch next to Zeus and me. "Put your feet here." He patted the spot where he wanted my feet.

Zeus urged me around, and I put my feet up where Thor patted.

"You want to be naked, baby?" Zeus asked.

"Yes," I whispered.

"Get her clothes off," Odin barked. "Let her feel his eyes on her."

Masculine hands began to pull off my outfit.

"You like a little danger, don't you, baby?" Odin said.

I nodded—it's the only answer I could give; the delicious feeling of their hands on me was taking up all my spare mental energy.

"You love to feel that edge."

Nod. Melt.

Thor started unbuckling my strappy shoes.

Odin growled a few threats at Denko.

I loved knowing he was there, So disapproving. So stern. His gaze was an accelerant, alcohol on flame.

So much hotter than I'd imagined.

I opened my eyes, and Thor leaned in for a kiss. "Oh my god, you love this," Thor said. "I can see from your eyes. You can feel him watching, and you love it."

Zeus bared a breast. My nipples felt rock hard, like I might come from just one touch, just one lick.

"Don't look at him," Odin said. "You can only at us." I turned to look at him as he touched me with utter possession, hands up and down my arms, hands on my neck. "Do you feel him, Ice? Can you feel his greedy eyes on you while we take you?"

"Yes," I said.

"This actually *is* kind of hot," Zeus breathed.

Odin said, "He wants to rob us of everything, but he only makes us stronger. And fucking hotter."

Zeus had my shirt all the way open. He pulled my bra cups down, forcing my breasts up and out, and brought his mouth near a nipple. "I want to feast on you."

But he didn't. He stopped with his mouth a millimeter from my needy nipple and said more stuff about how he wanted to feast on me. On and on, his breath tickled my nipple but didn't give me the touch I craved.

I hissed with need. "Please," I said.

"So greedy to come," said Odin.

A cloud of worry crossed my sex-addled brain. "What about ZOX?"

"You are safe, goddess," Odin said, sliding my hair behind my ears. "He told us that we have time." Odin slid his rough fingers along the tender shell of my ear. My libido skittered into overdrive, like it always did when he touched my ears. "Did you hear him? He talked about their tracking, *and* he talked about the hotel getting a bulletin. That gave it away."

"It did?" I panted.

"You are so sensitive here," Odin said.

"They wouldn't be sending bulletins to the hotels if they were really able to track us," Thor explained. "He was trying to scare us. Meaning we have time. Meaning if we want to make you wait forever to come while we take our sweet time sating ourselves on your body, we can."

"But we won't." Odin kissed my neck, creating wild electricity. Odin's possessive touch joined with the heat of Zeus's breath on my nipple, and the twin sensations jetted down to the sparkly party in my pussy.

I hissed in pleasure.

"Do you know how many false leads come from such a thing?" Odin said.

Was that even a question? Was he still talking about the bulletin somehow? I'd stopped listening.

Zeus pulled up my skirt.

"Many," Odin said.

"Okay," I said.

"Pull off her panties, Thor."

Thor pulled me off Zeus's lap. "On your knees." I got on my knees on the soft-as-butter couch as he pushed down my panties. I looked into his blue eyes, letting my nipples rub on his chest, a bit of rough with the soft.

Odin let me hands go. "Take down Thor's pants, goddess."

I took down Thor's pants, kissing him, rubbing against him. All of this sensation was too good, too much, and I wanted everything.

"You are going to bend over and take Thor all the way down your throat," Odin said. "Okay, baby?"

I inched back and complied.

He groaned as I took him, softly petting my hair. But it was too soft. In my watcher fantasy, they ravished me. Like, really fuck me like wild in front of the stern watcher. I pulled off and looked at him. "Can you," I said, "I mean..."

Thor's eyes went dark, and his fist flew to my hair. Thor, always on my wavelength. "Let's try that again," he growled, shoving my face into his cock while he pistoned his pelvis clear into my face. It was an amazing combination.

"That's it, goddess," I heard Odin say. I could feel fat, slickened fingers invading my ass. And right then I was gone in my mind.

Thor fisted my hair harder and clutched at my nipple with his other hand. I made a little sound.

"Not yet, Ice," Odin said. "Can you feel me in you? I'm going to shove my thick cock into your asshole. So far in. But not yet. Not until you're properly fucking Thor."

He directed Thor to pull out and lay back.

Thor let go of my hair and lay back. I pulled off him and wiped my mouth, looking down at his rosy, gleaming cock, swollen wild with veins.

"Come here," he said, so tenderly. "Crawl over me."

I crawled over him. Thor grabbed his cock and guided the thick knob of it to my sex, rubbing it up and down while Odin played with my breasts.

I thought I might cry for how badly I wanted to come.

"Fuck her, Thor, she can't last." Odin gave my ass a slap, and Thor pressed himself up into me, filling me. I could feel him so fat in me.

"Yes," he said, rocking gently. He placed his massive hands on my thighs where the stocking met the skin and rocked me into him, over and over. The world disappeared into sensation.

I felt a hand on my upper back. "You know what you have to do now, goddess," Odin said. "Bend over. Put your face into Thor's chest."

Thor stroked my hair gently, and this time I didn't stop him.

"Relax, goddess." Odin's impossibly thick cock nudged at my asshole.

"You feel so huge," I gasped. "So huge and good."

Thor stilled inside me. Odin grabbed my butt cheeks, massaging, making waves of feeling flow through me. I groaned, reeling.

"Take it, goddess." He pressed his huge girth into me, pistoning himself in, relentlessly invading me until both cocks were in me.

"Shit," I said, panting.

"Is that Mississippi?"

"God, no," I said. Mississippi was our stop word, and I was flying through the air, swinging from the moon. If anything, I wanted more.

"She loves when we use her hard," Odin said, moving wickedly inside me. Was he talking to Denko? Reminding me he was there? "It's like cutting the strings of a hot air balloon. She's almost gone. She's almost perfect. You can't believe how perfect she is." He slapped my ass. "Turn your head. Zeus needs his cock in your mouth."

Rough hands grabbed the back of my hair and turned my head. Zeus pressed his cock into me. "Uh-uh-uh."

And there were hands on my nipples and on my clit. I was spinning. I didn't know anything, except I was flying and spinning through the universe. It felt so good, being fucked into oblivion.

I didn't even know I was at the point of no return until Odin's voice broke through the fog in my brain. "She is so there." A hand caressed my back. "Do you feel it, baby?" With his other hand he clutched onto my hips and invaded me with force. "Do it, goddess, come for us."

"*Uh-uh-uh,*" Zeus said.

Thor groaned in that strangled way he had when he was on the verge. His cock swelled and vibrated inside me. Fingers dug into my hips.

I wasn't the only one gone, flying up and up.

But I didn't feel like a balloon, breaking its strings. I was more like a rocket ship, zooming up into the stratosphere, zooming up higher than ever, sensation building up and up.

If I was the rocket ship, I suppose my guys would be ground control, their huge massive cocks inside me, fucking me wildly and ruthlessly, which I'm pretty sure is not in the NASA manual. All the better.

And just like that I exploded into a zillion pieces—a zillion gravity-flouting, danger-defying pieces.

We collapsed on each other after, happy in our little world.

And Denko was out there, a cold moon.

Thor strolled across the room, hot and naked as a Greek Olympian, and started up the hot tub. He dipped in a toe. "Water's nice."

I moaned as Zeus picked me up, carried me over, and lowered me slowly in. Odin joined us.

"What did you think?" Zeus asked. "The watcher."

I looked over. Denko's stern eyes had followed us, of course.

"It was good," I said. "But I don't think it's an all-the-time activity. Eventually I forgot about him, and it was just hot when you used me for your complete and utter pleasure." I climbed into his lap. "Used me like a thing," I added wickedly.

Zeus sluiced the steamy water over my shoulders. "You're so far from being a thing to us. You are anything but."

Odin tipped his head back and gazed at the ornate ceiling. "Back to luxury hotels," he said softly.

"It's not so bad," I said. "This is actually one of the better hot tubs we've had, actually."

"You're starting to like Vegas, are you?" Zeus said.

"I'm starting to like it very much."

Thor pulled himself out and grabbed towels and hotel bathrobes for us all. Soon we were back on the couch in our snuggly and plush hotel robes digging into the feast from the sandwich cart—lots of really delicious fancy triangular sandwiches with sticks holding them together. On top of those sticks were little flags that said things like goat cheese and red pepper or ham and Swiss with caramelized onions.

"Hungry, Denko?" Zeus called out.

"I've lost my appetite," he called back.

Zeus shrugged.

Thor grabbed a tuna melt brioche triangle. In a low voice, he said, "We should rob a casino. You know, give Ice the full Vegas experience."

Odin snorted. "I'd want ten days to case a casino. At least."

"We'd have to case a casino just to figure out how to case it," Zeus said. "We don't have that kind of time. This was fun, but we can't be sloppy."

None of us said anything after that. He was right, of course.

It was time to work on an exit strategy.

Chapter Twenty-Four

THOR AND I GOT THE JOB OF BABYSITTING DENKO WHILE Odin and Zeus took the laptop in the other room to figure out where to go. They'd be using their ultra freak-out encrypted technology to purchase plane tickets in a way that couldn't be traced later, of course.

We were nomads again.

Thor turned on the TV and turned it so Denko could watch, too. Denko refused to give his vote on what we watched until Thor threatened him with more *Silver Spoons*, and we settled on *Die Hard 2*.

Odin took off to make arrangements, and Zeus joined us. At one point, they even agreed with Denko on a critique of how a bad guy would really set a trap.

"You guys didn't actually work together ever with Denko, did you?" I asked.

"Not directly," Zeus said. "Odin and I were in the field while he was still in training. Right? What year were you first in the field?"

"You really think this is going to work?" Denko said. "Your

days are numbered, and all the camaraderie in the world won't change that."

"Everyone's days are numbered," Thor growled.

"You picked the wrong team, Isis," he said.

"Seriously?" I said. "Have you been paying attention at all?"

Zeus sighed and held up a finger and a thumb. "Somebody is this close to duct tape on his mouth. *This close.*"

I leaned back against Thor and tried to concentrate on the show, but Denko had ruined it what with his death threats. My guys took it in stride, but I wasn't as hardened as they were. I wanted to ask that we switch the channel to something without explosions and gunfire, like maybe Oprah, but I didn't want to show Denko I felt insecure.

Odin came back with tickets and bags. It was time.

Thor made Denko get into a bed. He tucked him in and gave him a shot.

"Dead," Denko said. "You're dead."

We all stood around and watched the drug take him.

"Seven hours," Thor said. "Minimum. Maybe eight until he's conscious and calling attention to himself."

"Let's go, then," Zeus said. We had the room reserved for another day; it would be a healthy head start. We changed back into our street clothes, and my guys loaded up on the weapons. They made me put on my wig and skirt suit, which was surprisingly no worse for wear. I was shocked my guys hadn't torn anything.

We set out from our glorious hotel and split up. Zeus went off to see somebody about putting together a new Vegas go bag and stashing it. Thor went to get supplies and a car for the trip, and Odin mysteriously insisted I come with him. He hailed a cab.

"What's our job?" I asked Odin.

He leaned up and gave directions to the driver, then sat back. "A little bit of the Vegas experience before we go," he said.

"The casino?"

"No, no casino." He turned to me. "It was big, what happened today."

"I know," I said.

"I feel like we came through something. That's the thing about us. We come though things together. Help each other grow. And that thing between me and Zeus..."

"It was between me, too."

"I'm glad it's over."

"It's never over," he said. "I'll always have the history I do. So will Zeus. And you and Thor, too. It's just about staying vigilant. Our problems are lions guarding the gates of our love. It's up to us to fight through."

I kissed him. "I love that."

We pulled up in front of a Dunkin' Donuts. What? Odin was hungry again already? The Dunkin' Donuts stood between a pawnshop that was lit up like a Christmas tree and a wedding chapel, or the sort of over-the-top wedding chapel you hear about in Vegas; this one was a facsimile of a rural countryside wedding chapel, looking weirdly out of place with its plain white façade and peaked roof with a cross on the top. Though countryside chapels didn't typically have *Pastor Roger's Wee Chapel* painted above the door.

I eyed the donuts in the window as we stepped out. "I'm still full from our lunch," I said.

"Me too." Odin took my hand. "Come on." He led me down the sidewalk in the direction of the chapel...and up the steps.

"What are we doing?"

He turned to me at the top. "I'm thinking about the four of us. Forever."

"A wedding? Odin..."

"It's not legal, but..."

"You want the four of us to get married? Here? Now?"

He put a finger to my lips. "Keep the *four* part to yourself for now."

"What?" I laughed and grabbed his finger. "Odin, we're supposed to be escaping. Don't we have flights booked?"

"We have time."

"Odin..."

"I know we didn't ask you formally. We didn't ask each other either, but—"

"We don't have to ask. It goes without saying, but..." Heart pounding, I gazed up at the peak of the roof, an arrow into the blue, blue sky. "Getting married..."

Odin pulled me close and kissed my forehead. "Are you into it, baby?"

"Fuck yeah! But I'm..." I looked down at my outfit. "I'm in black."

"Not for long." He pulled me inside. We were expected.

Pastor Roger strolled up to greet us; the pastor was a deeply suntanned fiftysomething with bright white teeth and physique that suggested he did a lot more kneeling under a barbell than at an altar. The choirgirl with him looked suspiciously like an ex-show-girl what with her long, shapely legs sticking out from under a choir robe that was definitely shorter than what you'd see in an actual church. She looked me up and down. "Size ten. Come on." She led me into a side room stuffed with wedding gowns—beaded ones, princess ones, elegant hip hugging ones, strapless styles. It was a little bit...wonderful. "These are all tens."

"I don't understand."

"Pick one. Dress and tux rental is included with the price."

I was on those dresses instantly.

I pulled off my wig. We were going to do this right.

"Oh, good," she said. "I wasn't going to say anything, but ash brown is all wrong for you." With that she pulled out the perfect dress—a simple sleeveless gown of creamy white silk.

I gasped.

"I know, right? I'm like the dress whisperer. Put it on. Have you given thought to your vows?"

Vows. Was I ready for this? I tried it on. Perfect.

"Come on," she said. "Your wedding's in ten."

She led me out to a flowery little chapel area. *Goin' to the Chapel* was playing. And Odin stood there, devastating in his tuxedo.

"Goddess." He removed his glasses, slow and sexy. I could feel my face nearly splitting with a huge smile as I strode toward him, clutching my bouquet of white roses.

Just then, Zeus burst in. And looked at me. And stilled. "What's going on?"

"Get him a tux," Odin said.

"What are you doing?" Zeus said.

"We're getting married," Odin said. "The God Pack is getting married."

"What the hell?" Zeus said, long legs eating up the distance toward us.

"Is this your best man?" Pastor Roger said.

"Odin," Zeus said, going to Odin. "You didn't have to—"

"I did. I know it doesn't fix things for you, but I want you to see we're with you in everything."

"Brother." Zeus clapped Odin on the arm and turned around to me. "This is...I..." His green eyes shone. "You look beautiful," he whispered urgently, and then he yanked me to him and kissed me long and deep.

"Is he your...best man?" Pastor Roger asked with less certainty than before.

"Um..." It seemed a big thing to leave out, that four would be marrying.

"Get me a tux," Zeus said. "I'm ready."

"Only the groom gets the tux," Pastor Roger said.

Odin peeled off a wad of cash—a thousand bucks from the looks of it. "We're going to go for a nontraditional wedding."

Pastor Roger shrugged. "That'll rent him a tux."

I took Odin's hand at the altar. "Is Thor coming?"

Odin pulled his phone from his pocket. "He's supposed to be here."

"Do you have vows?" Pastor Roger asked.

Odin looked at me with a glint in his eye. Yes, we had vows. Odin always thought of everything.

"Rings?" Pastor Roger asked.

"Just placeholders," Odin said, pulling me roughly to him. "We'll steal you a real ring, later, baby. The ones you steal are always more beautiful."

Shivers went all over me. Could I love this man any more? Could I love any of them any more?

Pastor Roger didn't have a comment on whole stolen rings thing—or the make-out session with the best man.

Well, he was just lucky we hadn't brought a witness gagged and bound in a magician's cut-me-in-half box. Because that would definitely fly in the face of wedding etiquette.

Zeus strolled up looking like the most elegant secret agent ever. His smile took my breath away. About halfway down the aisle he slowed, as if to savor the moment. As if he'd been waiting forever for it.

"One more is coming," Odin said.

My choir showgirl looked at her wrist where a watch would be. "We have a service after yours."

Zeus came and stood on the other side of me, holding my hand.

Pastor Robert furrowed his brow. "When the actual ceremony starts, we'll want the best man off to the side."

Gulp.

"We all stand here," Zeus said.

Pastor Roger studied his face and seemed to decide that this best man could stand wherever he pleased. He too looked at his wrist where a watch would be—it seemed Pastor Roger's Wee Chapel had no shortage of imaginary watches. "We might have to start without your fourth."

"We can't," Odin said. "He's a groom."

"A double wedding?" Pastor Roger frowned. "This program is for one wedding."

"Not a double wedding, a single wedding with three grooms, one bride," Zeus said. "One wedding."

It took Pastor Roger a moment to digest this. "Wait, I can't marry four people."

Both Odin and I looked nervously at Zeus.

"I think you can," Zeus growled.

"I think..." I cut in, trying to sound reasonable, "I think... maybe you could make an exception?"

"I'm not marrying four people," Pastor Robert said. "It's not even legal. You can't just..." He trailed off, staring at Zeus warily.

"The four of us are a romantic unit," Zeus said. "We love each other, and we want to marry." He glanced over at me with a look of such intense love. I felt like the luckiest woman in the world, to have these fierce, amazing men to love.

Just then, Thor burst in.

"Quick, put him in a tux," Zeus said.

"That's illegal," the pastor said. "Even with the same-sex marriage act..."

But something was wrong. Thor was running down the aisle. "We have to go." He stopped at the altar, studying us with confusion on his face.

"What's going on?" Odin said.

Thor said, "I went back to the hotel to—" He glanced at Pastor Roger, then continued, "To get something out of the parking lot —and I noticed that the curtains to our room were open."

"We didn't leave them open," I said. Which meant somebody had gotten in there.

"You guys," Thor whispered. He took my hand. "Ice."

Odin strolled over to our hosts. "I think it goes without saying, Pastor Roger, that making a call to the police right now would not turn out well for you." He took the phone from the man's hand

and pocketed it. "Our reach and our power are awesome. You do not even want to know what would happen to you—"

The pastor held up his hands. "We're good. No calls."

Odin was already peeling off his tux jacket. "Have our clothes back here in two seconds, and you can keep the money."

"You guys." Thor arranged my veil around my shoulders. "This is...you *guys*. It would've been..." Thor was touched. Choked up.

"It would have been beautiful," I said.

Zeus looked so sad just then. This sort of thing meant so much to him. It *would've* been beautiful. Not legal, but beautiful.

"Hey." I held out my fist. "God Pack." Thor put his hand on mine, and then Zeus and Odin followed suit.

And then, with a crack in his voice, Odin said, "I promise to always love you. And protect you. And to fight for your dreams."

The vows.

Those were the vows he'd written.

"Let's go." Thor pulled away his hand.

"What the hell?" I grabbed his hand and put it back. I was the only girl and therefore apparently the only one to get weddings. I looked each one of my men in the eye and repeated the vow. "I promise to always love you. And to protect you. And to fight for your dreams." And then Thor said it, looking at each of us. Finally Zeus said it, voice cracking.

And it meant something up there on that altar in some fake chapel in that city full of fake things. One super-real thing: the four of us together, fighting for each other.

Only then did we break hands.

By the time we were in our underwear, our marriage helpers were back with the clothes.

We suited up, and two minutes later we were rolling tensely past glittering Las Vegas hotels in the white Firebird Thor had stolen. As usual, Zeus was driving, with Odin in front and Thor and me in the back.

It was a bit past rush hour. ZOX could be anywhere.

Shadows slanted over the glitz and glam and a very inconvenient traffic jam. We cracked the windows to let in the cool evening air, but not enough for people outside to be able to see us.

Thank goodness Thor had coveted this car and come back for it, or we'd still be in the chapel, unaware. Thor never could resist a classic muscle car. The tinted windows had probably put him right over the edge.

The traffic loosened up beyond the strip, but the tension didn't. We circled through the city and switched cars at a lot near the Vegas airport. Thor hated to lose the Firebird, but we had to be safe. We nabbed a Navigator and got on I-15.

"They got close," Thor observed as the Vegas suburbs gave way to desert.

"You wish we were dead, motherfuckers," Odin said.

Zeus's lips quirked.

I nestled into Thor's shoulder and gazed out at the salmon-and-orange-colored sky.

It felt good to be moving, but we couldn't relax quite yet; staying safe meant watching the mirrors and the traffic. It meant mile after mile of tense little exchanges—*What do you think of that black Volvo? Have we seen that Honda before? You want to pull off and lose the group?*

My guys needed sleep—desperately—but we probably wouldn't sleep until the plane.

But this was how we drove. This was how we rolled.

We were heading to Rome, Italy. Odin had arranged for three separate flights out of Salt Lake City following three different routes, just to break up the pattern.

It was full dark by the time we stopped for gas in Primm Valley. Thor and I headed to a strip of Western-themed shops to grab snacks. That's when I saw the bakery.

Cake. I snuck over and bought four pieces, each nestled in a fancy black box.

I broke them out once we were zooming back down the highway. "We didn't have a proper wedding, but we should still have cake." I handed them around. "Chocolate isn't a traditional wedding cake, but—"

"Chocolate is better," Thor said.

Odin turned in his seat. "I loved our wedding." He said it like a confession.

Zeus beamed in the rearview mirror. "I did, too. The traditional wedding was somebody else's wedding. But this one was ours. Better than what I could've dreamed."

"Me, too," I said.

We ate cake under the starry sky, not talking. Not needing to.

We just drove on and on into the night, hunted, exhausted, and dangerously in love, determined to love each other and protect each other and fight for each other's dreams.

Always.

~The End~

Thank you for being a guest at the wedding with the mostest!

&a.

But wait!!

The gang is in full honeymoon mode and Isis has never been happier...until tragedy strikes the family farm she had to leave behind.

People are dying...and her sister is being framed for murder!

Isis is desperate to save Vanessa, but how can she? It's too dangerous for her sisters to find out she's still alive, too dangerous for the gang to return to the scene of that crime.

At least that's what Thor and Zeus think.

But Odin's got other ideas.

Grab THE HARD WAY at your favorite bookstore!

Also by Annika Martin

THE BANK ROBBERS
Spicy reverse harem: read in order

The Hostage Bargain

The Wrong Idea

The Deeper Game

The Most Wanted

The Hard Way

The Best Trick

BILLIONAIRES OF MANHATTAN
Stand-alone romantic comedy: read in any order

Most Eligible Billionaire

The Billionaire's Wake-up-call Girl

Breaking The Billionaire's Rules

The Billionaire's Fake Fiancée

Return Billionaire to Sender

Just Not That Into Billionaires

Butt-dialing the Billionaire

DANGEROUS ROYALS

Dark and edgy mafia romance; read in order

Dark Mafia Prince

Wicked Mafia Prince

Savage Mafia Prince

Annika Martin writes in many genres; find a complete list of her books, audiobooks, and translated works at www.annikamartinbooks.com

All the Annika deets!

Annika Martin is a New York Times bestselling author who lives in Minneapolis with her non-bank-robber husband. In her spare time she enjoys taking pictures of her cats, consuming boatloads of chocolate suckers, and tending her wild, bee-friendly garden.

newsletter:
http://annikamartinbooks.com/newletter

TikTok:
@annikamartinauthor

Facebook:
www.facebook.com/AnnikaMartinBooks

Instagram:
instagram.com/annikamartinauthor

website:
www.annikamartinbooks.com

Reader group of awesomeness
www.facebook.com/groups/AnnikaMartinFabulousGang/

Q: Did the bank robbers leave you satisfied? Desperately yearning? Saddled with a mysterious cartoon porn addiction?

A. Whatever the answer, I'm always so grateful when people leave reviews, even just a line or two. It helps readers find the books and it super helps the series.

PS: Zeus sends kisses!

The bank robbers thank you for reading.